TRANSLATED FROM THE GIBBERISH

Also by Anosh Irani

NOVELS
The Cripple and His Talismans
The Song of Kahunsha
Dahanu Road
The Parcel

PLAYS
The Matka King
Bombay Black
The Men in White

TRANSLATED

FROM

THE

GIBBERISH

Seven Stories and One Half Truth

ANOSH IRANI

ALFRED A. KNOPF CANADA

PUBLISHED BY ALFRED A. KNOPF CANADA

Copyright © 2019 Anosh Irani

www.penguinrandomhouse.ca

Library and Archives Canada Cataloguing in Publication

Title: Translated from the gibberish :
seven stories and one half truth / Anosh Irani.
Names: Irani, Anosh, 1974- author.
Identifiers: Canadiana (print) 20190076194 | Canadiana (ebook) 20190076216 |
ISBN 9780735278523 (softcover) | ISBN 9780735278530 (HTML)
Classification: LCC PS8617.R36 T74 2019 | DDC C813/.6—dc23

Text and cover design: Jennifer Lum

Cover images: (suitcase) ©Sean Gladwell/Getty Images;
(ocean) ©Jiri Flogel/Shutterstock.com

Interior images: (boarding pass) © Nete/VectorStock

Printed and bound in Canada

2 4 6 8 9 7 5 3 1

Penguin
Random House
KNOPF CANADA

CONTENTS

TRANSLATED

FROM

THE

GIBBERISH

PART ONE

've been staring at the underwear hanging on the balcony opposite mine for several minutes now. It's old, it's tattered, it belongs to an elderly lady. A lady who happens to be deceased.

I am troubled, but it's not the underwear that's troubling me. My niggle is something else entirely.

It is the "I."

Who is this strange entity watching underwear flutter in the breeze? Is it me the writer, the narrator, the character? Is it an alternate consciousness without a body, single-minded in its pursuit of truth, or at least a story, gliding in and out of worlds both fictional and real only to disappear, once the writing is done, into the ether? It is perhaps this eye that I invoke now, this phantom "I" who happens to be gazing at the third-floor balcony of the flat belonging to Dr. Hansotia, now in his late seventies, a man who once had the love and respect of every person in Shapur Baug, the Parsi colony where I live.

The garment in question is large, like a bag you can hide something in. It is off-white, with a creamy hue much like the one that the pages of books acquire when left unread over time, or exposed to sunlight. Its elastic is worn; stretched beyond capacity, it has refused to snap back to its original circumference. The reason for this is not limited to the characteristics of cotton. There is an emotional, metaphysical explanation as well. After all, the owner of this underwear was Dr. Hansotia's wife of fifty years. With her gone, there is no reason for the elastic to snap back, just as there is no reason for Dr. Hansotia to continue hanging the underwear on the balcony a month after his wife's funeral. The underwear has thrown the residents of Shapur Baug into a tizzy. It is all they can speak about. *The doctor has lost his mind. He needs help. Someone needs to speak with him.*

Perhaps that is true. The mind can become unhinged after a singular traumatic event, or after a series of smaller traumas. But I think: The underwear hangs . . . and so what? It's not as if the doctor has put his wife's kidneys out to dry. I'm content to let the garment stay there. I'm closest to it in physical proximity, closer than any other resident in the colony. Therefore I feel I have more right to attack or defend it than the others.

EXHALE/EXILE

I once had a yoga teacher who would use the word "exile" when he meant to say "exhale." This was because of his accent. I was still in Bombay, before leaving for Canada twenty years ago. I had a perpetually blocked nose thanks to a deviated septum, and my family doctor—Dr. Hansotia—sent me to this man.

"Exile! Exile! Exile!" the teacher would say, letting out the breath from his belly and mouth at great speed, encouraging us to do the same. I found the idea of breathing in a closed space with fifteen other humans quite repugnant—all those germs moving around with the arrogance of frequent flyers, threatening to enter whomever they chose. But the word "exile" stayed with me, purely for its comic effect. Back then, I hardly knew what "exile" meant. Little did I know that the word would enter me more than any other germ, cause me to sneeze, writhe with fever, laugh, dance, dream, cry, do who knows what, as time went on, as a result of hurling myself from Bombay to Vancouver like a swashbuckling pirate. Now my swagger has gone, and I am as loose and unable to come back as Dr. Hansotia's wife's underwear.

Some time ago, I came upon this passage by Edward Said:

> *Exile is strangely compelling to think about but terrible to experience. It is the unhealable rift forced between a human being and a native place, between the self and its true home: its essential sadness can never be surmounted. The achievements of exile are permanently undermined by the loss of something left behind for ever.*

This is a terrible piece of writing. Terrible in its truthfulness, in the feeling it evokes, in its ability to both ask a question and then conclude, without question, that there is no solution to its pain. It left me feeling weak and angry. I have been moved by literature time and again, inspired by its awesome power, such as when I first read *A Fine Balance* by Rohinton Mistry, or Flannery O'Connor's "A Good Man Is Hard to Find," or Zora Neale Hurston's *Their Eyes Were Watching God.* These are stories that contain truths. This passage, however, was truth that told a story, my story. And I couldn't bear to hold it in my hands. Twenty years of being in a foreign land, and instead of gaining something, I was being told that I had lost?

I cannot remember my yoga teacher's face. At least, not entirely. I remember his nostrils and his mouth. But not the eyes.
He almost never opened his eyes. I have a feeling he was from
Kerala, and was stuck in Bombay. He was expressing, through
his nostrils, what Said had written. The self and its true home
were so far apart that only breathing could calm him down,
smooth out his anxiety. I didn't know at the time that he was
offering me a tool, a coping mechanism that I could use in
Canada. Dr. Hansotia hadn't sent me to him because of my deviated septum. He'd sent me to this man because he somehow
knew that my leaving India was going to cost me much more
than international student fees.

"Why are you going?" he asked me, when I went to his clinic
for a final checkup just before I left. I still remember the day
and date. August 11, 1998. It was a Tuesday. I was set to leave for
Canada a week later.

"I'm going there to study," I said.

"Study what?"

"Er . . . creative writing."

"You want to be the next Tennessee Williams?"

"No," I said. "I mean . . ."

"Son, are you sure you want to become a writer?"

A writer? Who said anything about becoming a writer?
What the hell was this guy talking about? But of course, secretly,
that's what I had decided. I just had no intention of announcing
it. To anybody. To say it would make it real. This was my dirty
little tryst with destiny. Perhaps, back then, I didn't understand
the seriousness of my undertaking—I was about to lock horns
with something that was larger than me, more powerful, and

completely dangerous. I was on my way to becoming a flammable object. That's what writers are. And I knew I had it in me, this innate ability to combust.

Writing isn't about prose. It's not about stories, plots, characters, themes, images, ideas, and, certainly, not about redemption. Do you have the ability to combust? To fucking implode time and again, day in and day out, with the stamina of an athlete, until you have written that novel of yours? Once the book is out, even if it gets great reviews, this still doesn't prevent your nerves from being on fire, because the next story has already come along, it's already spewing and vomiting inside your gut —it knows that your ability to combust is far greater than your capacity to heal.

Maybe Dr. Hansotia saw that in me, much more than I did at the time. I was, as they say, full of the arrogance and exuberance of youth. And in the three years since I had graduated from university with my B.Com. (Bachelor of Complacency), I had grown shadowy. I no longer lived in the light. I stopped playing football, stopped going to nightclubs, avoided large crowds, felt pissed off hearing laughter. I just stayed at home and stared out my window into the dark, at the glow of lumber mills and cooking fires. But I wrote nothing. I didn't know how to. I was seething, the fury was building, and I had to leave. That's all I knew. *Leave.* If I had stayed on any longer in Bombay, I would have had a motorcycle accident, or gone to the red-light district and smashed a pimp's head with a bottle.

"Just make sure you do yoga," said Dr. Hansotia. "Keep doing it even there, it will help you." In other words, make sure you breathe.

"Yes," I said.

As soon as I landed in Vancouver, I inhaled. On that very first day, I took such a deep breath that my lungs were shocked by the purity of the air, the sheer audacity of oxygen. I continued doing yoga breaths for a few days. Then I told myself that if this was the quality of the air around me, I wouldn't need yogic breathing. After Bombay's smoke-filled, polluted death offering, this Vancouver air seemed like a trick.

It was. And I fell for it.

TWENTY YEARS LATER, I SIT by the window in the very room where I grew up. It's dark outside, the only light coming from a small cooking fire in the lumber mill visible through my window. This is not a typical Bombay view—there are no vehicles, no smoke clouds, no skyscrapers. Just low tin roofs that stretch out for hundreds of metres. In the distance, there is a small building near a cemetery. More space, the dead laid out horizontally for my benefit, not blocking the view. If you think about it, bodies should be buried vertically, to save space. At least, that's how I would do it. This is what I think about at night. I cannot blame the jet lag. I wouldn't call myself an insomniac, but sleep and I have a tumultuous relationship. Or perhaps, like so many relationships, it's one-sided. I love it, but it doesn't love me back, and what I'm left with is thoughts of vertical burials. My friends tell me that I'm morbid. Why do I think of these things? But if not vertical burials, what? The stock market? Bank statements, families, children, picnics, weddings? No, thank you. Vertical burials need some pondering.

The thing is, something keeps me up at night, whether I'm in Vancouver or Bombay, and I know what it is—or what they are—but I can't catch them, I cannot exhume them. They are fragments of something deeply embedded in my consciousness. They are all this back-and-forth between continents and cultures, for two decades now, and my inability to own a home, to find a home, to feel at home. Exhale/Exile. Vertical burials. A woman's undergarment. All gibberish, really. But they make it impossible for me to sleep. And so I have come to the conclusion that nights are not for sleeping. Nights are for translating.

I recently had the pleasure of reconnecting with my Italian translator, Anna Rusconi. On the topic of translation, she mentioned that she doesn't like to "touch the body" too much. In other words, a translator is not a scientist who examines the text with a scalpel. She simply stands next to the work, really close, "feels its breath, and understands it as though heat is being exchanged by two people who are very close to each other." My body is exuding these fragments of consciousness into the air, but there is no one but me to intercept them, catch them. I am my own translator, my own doom.

I move to the other side of the apartment, to the row of sliding windows near the main door. My parents are asleep in their room, at the opposite end of the apartment. They are sleepers. No fragments, no translating. While they sleep the sleep of kings, I stare at the underwear. The garment is so motionless that I'm afraid it will come to life any moment, and smother me because I'm staring at it. What a marvellous death that would be.

   – How did he die?
   – Oh, by underwear.
   – By underwear? What do you mean?

– He was staring at a dead woman's underwear, and it
suddenly sprang to life and smothered him.

I would insist on being buried vertically, with the underwear in my mouth. Halfway down my throat, the rest of it rising like sour milk in a horrible puff.

I light a cigarette just to burn the taste of the underwear. It's the lighting of it, and that first drag, that I enjoy. The rest gives me a headache. But what else can one do at night? How many almonds can one eat, how many cups of tea—green or otherwise? It's fine; it will be morning soon. Soon, I will hear the sound of the newspaper being tucked into the space between the door and the latch, and the nation's news will find its way into our home, where it will mix with tea and curdle everything it touches.

Now that the morning light is about to enter, I go back to my room, and close my eyes. The three hours or so of sleep that I get will be full of dreams. More unnecessary fragments. My most recent one: I saw a black-and-white photograph of a man's face. Below it, his name, Sitar K., written in pencil. He used to work in a circus. Then, another drawing—an architectural sketch of the circus. Someone had drawn an arrow and scribbled the following words in pencil: *This is the spot from which he fell and died.* Translation: not a clue.

The next morning, I google "Sitar K." Nothing. Then, "Sitar K. + Circus." Nothing. I google my dreams. Should I consider myself lucky? That I have the time? That I don't, or choose not to, rush to an office and sit in a cubicle, which is just another version of a grave?

The doorbell rings. I take my ashtray to the door and empty it into the garbageman's cane basket; it's full of half-smoked cigarettes, a healthy, expensive way of smoking. My next-door neighbour greets me with a big hug and a kiss. She asks me, as she always does when she sees me, if I am *finally* married. In my mind I tell her, as I always do, that I would prefer a vertical burial, while I am alive, to the M-word. But she's elderly. So I just nod and tell her, "Soon, soon." Then she tells me about Dr. Hansotia's wife. "She used to be my childhood friend," she says. "The three of us, Hosi, me, and her, used to be in the same school."

I know that already. I have known since I was a child. But I let her speak. Sometimes old people need to speak. The bodily muscles no longer move much, but the tongue moving makes them feel muscular. I let her feel muscular.

"It's just awful what happened to her."

"What happened?" I ask.

"She died of a brain tumour. And that son of hers didn't even come to see her."

That I did not know. It's not what I would have expected of Yezdi. The last I heard, which was several years ago, he was in Silicon Valley.

"That's why I'm saying get married quickly," she tells me.

So that I have a son and he *doesn't* show up when I'm dying? I say it was great to see her, and start to move back towards my door.

"And that underwear," she says. "That underwear . . ."

"What about it?"

"How dare he . . . that is Jaloo's personal . . . I told him what I thought, but he just nodded. He has lost his mind."

Wouldn't anyone? If your childhood sweetheart, your wife of fifty years, is gone, and your only child doesn't come to visit, wouldn't you lose your mind too? Shouldn't that be the primary concern for my neighbour? For everyone?

Once I am back inside the apartment, I look at the undergarment again. I love the word "undergarment." A garment, according to the dictionary, is simply an item of clothing. But add the word "under" to it and the wheels of outrage start to turn. For a deeper understanding of the word "undergarment," I turn to Wikipedia (as one should for a reliable account of anything):

> *Undergarments are items of clothing worn beneath our outer clothes, usually in direct contact with the skin . . . They serve to keep outer garments from being soiled or damaged by bodily excretions, to lessen the friction of outerwear against the skin, to shape the body, and to provide concealment or support for parts of it.*

Now that Jaloo's body is gone, what is the underwear doing? It's creating a ruckus in the minds of my neighbours. But what's it doing for Dr. Hansotia? Or to him? He doesn't go out much anymore, according to my father. He gave up his practice a while ago, and now he just sits at home. My head starts to hurt. I go to my room, shut the door, pull the blinds down, turn the fan to full speed, and let the dust enter my nostrils. The histamines in my body are now going berserk, my eyes are red, I sneeze and I feel choked up. There's no question I'm home.

TENNESSEE WILLIAMS

When Tennessee Williams's lover died of a brain tumour, Williams expressed it thus: "An awful flower grew in his brain."

As I stand by the window at night, and stare at the underwear again, I think of the first time I read that name. It was through the glass of Dr. Hansotia's bookcase. I was in grade five or six, and I had gone over to his home to apologize to his son, Yezdi, for teasing him about a particular girl. All I had done was tell Yezdi that he was in love. That was all. And it had made him cry. It had terrified him, but I had no idea why. When I went to his house, he refused to come out of his room. His mother, Jaloo aunty as I called her, went to fetch him, and I was left seated with Dr. Hansotia in the living room. We sat in silence. It was then that I read the name Tennessee Williams. I must have tilted my head to read it along the book's spine, because Dr. Hansotia asked me what I was looking at.

He then walked over to the bookcase, took the book out, and caressed its cover with so much care that I thought Williams must be a doctor. But his book didn't look like a medical book. There was a plastic cover—to preserve the original—put on by Dr. Hansotia himself, I assumed; it looked like his work, so precise and surgical. He tried to explain what the book contained or what it meant to him, but I was too young to understand. I only remember the look on his face. There was such longing in it; there was admiration, envy perhaps, and a deep sadness. When I think about it now, it was as though he was touching Mr. Williams's face, removing his glasses, cleaning them for him, performing some small duty that only a disciple could. I wonder if he still has that book. I wonder if he feels one way or the other about the fact that the love of his life, like Tennessee Williams's love, died of that "awful flower."

Tonight, I decide to translate another fragment.

A fragment from Canada. A year ago, I lost someone close to me, a person whom I had met not more than fifteen times in my entire life. And yet the hole, the one she has excavated within me, is so vast that I can only fill it with gratitude, nothing else. Perhaps that was her plan all along. Not just for me, but for all those she dug into.

Her name was Iris. And she was my dramaturge.

But Iris was no ordinary dramaturge. She could really *see* —the play itself, and the soul behind the play. After all, that was why she was named Iris. "Yes, asshole," she would tell me. "But that's not what the play's *about*." Then, through the haze of cigarette smoke that surrounded her, came this beautiful clarity. All those months spent in isolation, all those darkened rooms and doubts, were bathed in this light, thanks to her. Eventually, flowers grew in her too. But not in her brain.

Tonight, I light up in her honour. Oh, how she would have hated that word. "Just smoke. And get it over with!" would have been her advice. But I have nights to counter. I have the night to live through, inch by inch. I don't lie still in bed. I crawl. I crawl like a worm from one end to the other, hoping to find something. The very thing that Iris found time and again, the thing behind the thing. From a young age, I've been after life itself: what's behind you? You can't be it. There has to be more. These balloons, picnics, jobs, salaries, exams, wars, riots, puppies, husbands, wives, partners—and more balloons. I mention balloons twice only because as a child I'd release them and watch them fly away and wonder where they went. What disturbed me was that no one else seemed concerned about their fate. Screw the cake; what happened to that poor balloon?

More fragments. I leave the house, walk down the stairs in the dark.

Where once there was plain grass in the rains and dry earth in the summer, there is now a children's playground. It used to be a haven for us when we were kids: we played football, cricket, a game called hitty-kitty where you formed a human chain. There would be two teams of six or seven each. One guy would lean against a parked car or a wall for support, his back flat, his knees slightly bent, then another would stand behind him in that same position, his arms circling the waist of the guy in front, his head to the side, and another would stand behind him, and so on. The opposite team would take a long run, speeding towards the chain, thumping on his back the guy on the end, then flying into the air to land as far forward as possible, with a huge thud. The idea was to make the other team collapse under the weight. This was the whole point —and it was marvellous. I imagine playing it in Canada and chuckle. And I wonder how none of us, as children, got spinal cord injuries. Not one of us received a scratch. Sometimes we'd hear something crack, but we brushed it off, figuring it was a nearby twig, not someone's vertebrae. It was all in a day's play. Even back then, Yezdi would cry. Once, as he was standing with his back flat in the chain, the guy in front of him, his own teammate, farted in his face and the whole chain collapsed laughing. Now I wonder, was he crying for his mother who would die years later? Or for his father who was perhaps disappointed in him? Or for the fact that he hated India and his friends and always wanted to leave? Was the fart in his face life itself, that thing behind the thing, which trumpeted his future without warning?

I walk around in the dark, circle the playground of my past, the way I've always imagined Edward Albee circled his typewriter each morning before he started writing. There's something about this playground that I need to write about. I haven't found it yet. I look up at the surrounding buildings: C Block, D Block, E Block. A couple of lights are on, some air conditioners are whirring. I stare at the underwear again. I wonder if any pubic hair is still stuck to it. A fragment, nothing more. I wonder what would happen if I were to actually reveal this thought to someone, express it out loud. Would I ever get another Canada Council grant?

In your final report, please state the research you undertook for your short story collection.

Sure. I walked around in the dark and stared at a dead woman's underwear.

Okay. We wish you the best in your future endeavours. Please do not contact us again.

This is what my MFA in creative writing has resulted in. I feel for my parents. My father had to sell off his old Jeep for my plane ticket. All I had when I arrived in Canada was enough money, barely, to survive for six months. A note to young people: Please think hard before pursuing a career in the fine arts. There's nothing fine about it. All things fine—fine wine, fine food, fine homes, fine cars, fine art, especially fine art—are enjoyed by other people, people who listen to their parents and to society. Become doctors, lawyers, accountants, RMTs, bankers, politicians, whatever, and *then* keep Tennessee Williams in your bookcase, first editions, signed by the master himself.

Sometimes I think of suicide, but there's always that next sentence. There's always that next image. I'm being fed lines, like an IV drip over a hospital bed that prolongs suffering, not life. Something tickles my brain in the most tantalizing way, then disappears. And I know that my next book has begun.

There's something about this playground. I keep circling.

I see something move, right above the underwear. It's Dr. Hansotia. He's by the window, three floors up, staring out into the sky. He hasn't seen me. I know I shouldn't wave. That would be too jarring. So I cough. The night is quiet, and maybe he'll realize I'm here, just like him, trying to find something. But he does nothing. He's as still as a bat now.

The next thing I know, I'm walking up the stairs again. His stairs. It's 3 a.m., but who cares? He's up, I'm up. I go to the third floor. It's been more than twenty years since I've stood at this door. It's still the same, with the same dull nameplate: *Hansotia*. I knock on the door with my knuckles. The doorbell would shatter the moment. It's hardly audible, my knock. Even to me. I wait. Nothing. I wonder what I'm doing. I can see my apartment window from here. That window looks so pointless, like a rectangular hole in concrete, like a photograph, and I see what Dr. Hansotia must have seen from his window, a little boy who was once happy, played sports, studied, ate raw mangoes dipped in chili powder, then became a hormonal youth and started wearing tight clothing, followed by extra-loose clothing, then grew a strange moustache because he was hairy, then shaved it for the first time, read only Amar Chitra Katha comics, Tintin, Asterix and Obelix, and could have cared less about the Hardy Boys and Enid Blyton—thought they were dull, so dull that he was forced to imagine a colour that didn't exist—then fell ill, grew moody, irritable, stood at the window again, but was no longer the same boy who had once stood there, then left for Canada, came back intermittently, looked even more confused, went back, came back, continued this placement and displacement for two decades, and now, finally, all that was left was a rectangular hole in a four-storey concrete building, nothing more, in which a living ant, a miniature, insignificant insect, had played out some shitty short film, one that had some moments but lacked unity as a whole, and as the camera zooms back to take the landscape seventy-millimetre shot, I see thousands of windows, the whole city of Bombay, the whole of Mumbai, a city with two names and twenty million souls, all performing in the dark, only a fraction of them realizing they are nothing more than petty cash.

I knock again. This time, I put some weight behind it.

After a few seconds, I hear the slow shuffle of feet, the sound that old people make when they go to the toilet in the middle of the night, muscles not quite awake, feet unable to lift, or perhaps not lifting on purpose, staying close to the ground because they know that's where they're headed. The shuffle stops. I know Dr. Hansotia is on the other side.

He opens the door, just a crack. He says nothing.

"Hello, Doctor," I say. "It's me."

He doesn't look at my face. He looks at my chest for some reason. Still, silence.

"I just wanted to offer my condolences," I continue. "I saw you were awake . . ."

More silence. Then he shuts the door on me. It's not rude; it's like a slow curtain closing. He's allowed my condolences to enter, a whiff, but not me. I don't even hear the door click. I stand there and stare at my feet. I wonder why humans do this, stare at their feet when things go wrong. Am I blaming my feet for bringing me here? Up these stairs? Then I should be blaming my hands too, for writing, for doing that most ridiculous of things, making me believe I was of value, had something special to offer. Shouldn't I blame my hands for holding books, realizing their power, allowing their electricity to enter my body and brain? Why just the hands, though? The eyes as well, for seeing. For seeing things in a strange and wobbly light.

EAR, NOSE, AND THROAT

There is something to be said about the human body. From the time we are little, we are always being told that we need to look after it. Health is wealth. Without your health, you have nothing. And where does this health reside? In the human body.

The body is present everywhere, even in literature. We call a writer's work a body of literature. One of the most beautiful pieces of writing that I have come across has to do with the body —the opening page of Marguerite Yourcenar's novel *Memoirs of Hadrian*, written as a letter from Hadrian to his successor, Marcus Aurelius. Hadrian speaks of a visit to his physician Hermogenes, and how the latter was "alarmed" at the sight of the emperor's body, and the "rapid decline" of his health. Hadrian writes:

> *It is difficult to remain an emperor in presence of a physician, and difficult even to keep one's essential quality as a man . . . This morning it occurred to me for the first time that my body, my faithful companion and friend, truer and better known to me than my own soul, may be after all only a sly beast who will end by devouring his master.*

Naked before his physician, Hadrian suddenly feels like a child, a slave, a patient, a worthless, weakened reptile. And his impending doom towers above him, just as I tower above the reptile that I have killed in my room tonight—a lizard. Again I am not able to sleep, and the white tube lights in my room give off a subway station glow, as if underground. For the past three nights a lizard had been gliding along my window, its belly pressed flat against the other side of the glass as it moved back and forth, sometimes slowly, sometimes rapidly.

At night, I keep the window closed. There are too many reptiles, insects, bugs—winged creatures that believe they have the right to enter my room just because they have wings. I would like to tell them that angels have wings too, and angels have been banished, sent into exile. But it's hard for me to get through to the insects and reptiles. My father, on the other hand, does not believe in communication. He simply reaches for the cockroach-killing repellent and sprays the entire room with it. Bugs, mosquitoes, and lizards fall from the ceiling of my room like dead stars. My pillows smell of repellent, and I get hit by it, too, an extra surge of chemicals to keep me awake. The fan above me whirs, another winged creature, angrily spinning in the same cycle again and again. I sweat with anxiety and heat. It is on nights like these when I long for Canada. Not so much for its vast open spaces, but for a particular recreation centre in North Van, and its freshly minted pool, where I spend evenings doing laps and breathing hard: exile, exile.

As I lie in my Bombay bed, I start doing the butterfly stroke, I make the white sheets turn blue and sink into the water. I drop into another dimension and observe creatures like myself who think their bodies mean something. The pool is the best place to observe humiliation and decay, hubris and illusion.

Between laps, I look around and ask myself, "What are we?"

We are flesh on vertebrae. That's about it. And yet we refuse to see that. Young men with rippling abs glide through the water like emperors, without the slightest clue that one day they too will meet their Hermogenes; then there are the old men—white, brown, hairy, scary—who feel power surge through their bank accounts even while they are one step away from using shit bags.

The water is trying to tell us the truth by shrivelling our skin, but no one pays attention. Water, that most truthful of things. We drink it, it keeps us clean, but we do not allow it to keep us honest. Swim for an hour. Look at your finger; those concentric shrivelled circles, that's the truth circling around us, trying to find a way in. But all we do is dry off and put on a thick layer of cream.

I often watch one man—I think he is Iranian—who has a full mane of back hair. He swims beautifully, and his hair swims along with him, behind him, but almost separately, wavy strands creating a jazz riff through the water. I sometimes think I would like to buy him a pair of scissors or a razor, but then again, perhaps he is wiser than the rest of us—he is allowing himself to turn into a root, or the side of a hill; he is ready to return to the earth.

The lane to the extreme right is the slow lane. It should be renamed the bobbing lane—everyone in this lane bobs up and down in the water, following the instructions of a fitness expert who has promised them . . . something. Everyone tries so hard to maintain the body, to keep it going. Health is wealth. And apparently, judging from what can be seen at the pool, the exact place where health resides in the human body is in the butt.

Butts jut out of swimming costumes, restrained by fabric from falling to the floor. But I say they should fall to the floor and slide away from us entirely, where they will merge with other butts, and the collected mass of butt jelly will make its way past the reception area of the rec centre into the concrete parking lot, then cut across lawns, through a wedding ceremony whilst the couple is exchanging vows, then over concrete again, over buildings, over that ugly mass of unaffordable Vancouver housing, and finally into the beloved Pacific Ocean.

But no, we love our gluteus muscles more than we love our own children; we give them the care they so desperately need in order to keep them close to us, proud and shapely. We imprison them in our underwear, so that they stick to our bodies; we trap them in jeans and tights. In our next incarnation, I propose, we should all be born without arses. Nothing but flat skin, like the top of a butter block.

Dr. Hansotia's wife had a butt too, and underwear once carried it, contained it. Now that container is the cynosure of all eyes. I'm done with my laps now. I'm done thinking about underwear. I beg for sleep, I pray for it the way a farmer prays for rain. I exhort the gods to provide me with it. I invoke them by closing my eyes, and I hear the ceiling fan cutting the air. Quincy Jones has said that he likes to compose music at night. That's when it's quiet, he said, and he always leaves room for the Lord to come in. That's how the magic happens.

I don't write music. But writing itself is musical, it's about rhythm. It is contained in the body, essentially. The stories that I will tell ten years from now are already embedded in my DNA, and they will erupt when they need to. There it is again, the body. It is useful, but it needs to know its place, it cannot have so much power over me. Again, the body is keeping me awake, staying up when it needs to stay down. If sleep is so crucial for the body, shouldn't there be a switch? Switch on, switch off. Simple. But perhaps the lack of a switch is the human struggle.

As a writer, I'm constantly trying to remember. As a human being, I'm trying to forget. Sleep is that in-between state, between remembering and forgetting, where water, the eternal truth-teller of which we are made, swims around within us, nudges our organs, and tells our bodies exactly what to remember and what to forget—so that my remembrances become fictions, and my forgetfulness makes me human, brings me peace. But I remember everything.

And so, like Quincy, I leave room for the Lord to come in.

I open the window. But there is no Lord; instead, a lizard enters. Perhaps she is looking for her son; a mother coming into my room and shuddering that her little one is gone.

LANGUAGE

Immigrants speak in fragments. This is their language of choice —or rather, this is the language that has been chosen for them. Incoherence. The inability to understand, to be understood. Ask immigrants where they are from, ask the question, "So what is home for you?" and you will see the agony on their faces. Of course, as a writer, I get asked that question all the time, and it is a valid one, and I answer it without missing a beat: I have two homes, and I have neither. That is what I say in interviews. But catch me off guard, catch me at a train station in Bombay, or when I am staring into someone else's home from a bridge, and you will see the lines appear on my face.

As my neighbour did this morning. I was emptying my trash into the garbageman's cane basket, and she asked me, "Do you like it there?"—meaning my other home, Vancouver—and I said, "Sure, sure," and she said, "It must be so clean," and I said, "Yes, yes," and just as I was about to re-enter my apartment, she asked, "So, are you happy there?" and the truth is a resounding no, but then I'm not happy here either, because there is no here, here *was*, it no longer *is*, and it's questions like these that keep pharmaceutical companies in business. Am I happy anywhere? Was I ever happy? Is there such a thing as happy? I don't think so, and if there is, I don't want it. I want to combust in such a powerful way that the effects are felt deep in the oceans; I want craniates to read my work and get my meaning, and that's about it. It won't make me happy, but it will give my combustion the distance it deserves.

While I'm feeling all this, my neighbour tells me that she went over to Dr. Hansotia's place and rang the doorbell but he didn't answer. What if he's dead? What if he's had a stroke and is just lying there on the kitchen floor? But then, upon further investigation, she discovered that he has been opening the door for the garbageman, and has also hired a new maid to help cook, clean, and get groceries. So he has every intention to live. My neighbour seems a bit disappointed by this. Just as I'm disappointed by my constant need to make sense of a decision I made twenty years ago—to leave. I can feel my body turning dark; I can feel an eclipse occurring within me, the light being blocked.

Over the next few days, I keep one eye on Dr. Hansotia's window as I do my regular Bombay things—I visit friends' homes, try to partake of the natural rhythms of their daily lives: their morning jogs, afternoon naps, shopping trips (oh, how the malls have grown; they are the Great Barrier Reefs of our age), domestic arguments, laughter that I hear and remember from long ago, lovers who have aged and seem "happy," money flowing in and out of wallets and cards, and me, reaching into my wallet to pay for dinners only to be scoffed at, but in the most affectionate way, because I am an artist, an adorable pye-dog. So many natural, daily rhythms that seem completely unnatural to me, such as sharing space with another human being; waking up next to one; having a miniature version of oneself and then holding it, scolding it, cuddling it, cleaning it. Once in a while, someone hands me their baby, hoping it will change me, hoping that some of its babyness will redeem my soul, make me less grouchy, or whatever it is they think I need. This obsession with happiness—to me it's just a new-car smell that one day disappears without warning. I try to partake of daily life, but I find natural rhythms only when I am writing. But I cannot write all the time. So I think.

It's 2 a.m. A peaceful time to be awake in Bombay. I still call the city Bombay when I speak, but I've started using Mumbai when I write. Mumbai is creeping into my work. Those seven islands are speaking up, telling me it's time to acknowledge the name change. If it's only a name change, I tell those islands (when you're up four days in a row, you can communicate with islands), why is it so difficult for me to say it? Is it because when I say Mumbai I don't know where to go? Or is it because Mumbai has no use for me, doesn't need me the way I need it? On my previous trip, a year ago, I went to Chowpatty beach at night and dipped my feet in the sea. And just as I started to feel the warmth of the water, the water tightened its grip around my ankles and I realized that water, that eternal truth-teller, was back at work. *You did not leave Bombay,* the water said. *It spat you out. Remember this, each time you hold that new passport of yours.* When I returned to Vancouver, I dipped my feet in the waters of English Bay, thinking I would spite the Arabian Sea. But the Pacific had a message for me as well. Not so much in words, but in its cold, steely silence.

In Bombay, once I'm done holding other people's babies and shopping, once I'm done catching up with friends or watching a Hindi movie in Phoenix Mills, I do something strange—strange to others but not to me. I take late-night taxi rides alone. Even though people offer to drop me home after our nights out, I prefer cabs. There's a bridge in the city, the JJ Bridge, which connects Byculla, the place where I live, to Colaba in South Bombay. At night, when there's no traffic, it's just a ten-minute ride between those areas, and I use that bridge to stare into homes, into people's apartments, to catch a glimpse of the smallness of their movements, to see complete strangers perform mundane acts such as reaching for a newspaper, or to watch an old woman fanning herself. The bridge allows me to be so close to their windows that I can literally smell their lives. This is an essential part of my Bombay visit. As my taxi climbs up that bridge, I feel a kind of exhilaration—perhaps that's too grand a word: a release, you might say. I become an eagle who swoops in and out of lives, of narratives, without the slightest regard for plot or character development. I collect snapshots, take photographs in the mind with eye blinks, in order to find the thing behind the thing, which I hope will enlarge my world; and when I do find that moment, I don't know what to do with it. The second I begin to feel complete, to fill up with something, a sense of loss pervades me. Then I stop looking into apartments, I look below the bridge, at Mohammed Ali Road, at its mosques and minarets, its greenness, its lights sending out signals into the sky, and it feels like an ancient place, a place that contains the breath of centuries, warm and stale. I fill my nights with domes in the sky, and minarets, with roundness and erectness, and this says a lot about how I feel about Earth itself—that I am stuck in its roundness, when all I long for is upward movement, a minaret that will take me so high . . . And my thoughts stop as soon as I descend the bridge and pass by my old school—or, specifically, the petrol pump behind my school. When childhood memories take over, it's time for me to leave.

It took me many visits to India, many taxi rides across the JJ Bridge, before Canada made its appearance, before it intercepted me, the way a train switches tracks and suddenly you are off course, or so you think—but you're really going where you were headed all along. There's something about the Lions Gate Bridge in Vancouver that has always bothered me, but I didn't understand what it was until one night on the JJ Bridge. I'm always being told by people who visit Vancouver how stunning it is, how lucky I am to live here/there. When people from India come here, they say, "It's jannat." This is heaven, this is paradise. For a second, I am filled with some sort of pride, but this quickly goes away. I digress. And I digress because that's what the Lions Gate Bridge is: a digression. The opposite of focus. If the JJ Bridge in Mumbai allows me to focus, to stare into windows, into tiny lives, the two lions at the mouth of the bridge in Vancouver tell me that something regal is at hand, something majestic—and at first, you buy it. You stare at the North Shore Mountains, at those homes in North and West Vancouver that

almost seem to touch the sky and the water and the clouds all at
once, and you take a deep breath, and it's invigorating. And that's
what I did, too, until one day I looked down *below*, and realized:
I don't know a thing about these people. And by "these people"
I mean the people whose land this actually is, these people who
live on reserves *below* the bridge, underneath the bridge, as life
passes them by above, as we move above them, in machines, full
throttle, so fast that we fail to pay attention, fast because we don't
want to pay attention, or have been trained not to. Shouldn't
these reserves below the bridge be in the sky—not to elevate
them to the status of legend and myth, because that would once
again diminish the real history—but so that we notice them?

In 2003, I took an oath to become a Canadian citizen. I went
to the ceremony alone, on a weekday, and stood with another
group of people, most of them recent immigrants, I assumed,
and listened to a judge talk about Canada. I still remember parts
of what he said. How Canada was this great mosaic, this tapestry
of cloth made up of different peoples, and now I was being asked
to contribute to it, become part of it. And then, this particular
phrase: "I invite you to insert your thread into the Canadian
tapestry." For some reason, I got the giggles. I would love to
insert my thread, I thought. I looked at those next to me to see
if anyone else found these words funny. Not so. There was an
Asian woman looking directly at the judge as though she was
worried she would be thrown out of the country if she did not
behave; there was, to my left, someone whose face I cannot remember, because I kept asking myself, as I looked left and right,
Where are those people from under the bridge? Why aren't they
here, as representatives of this great land, to welcome, to educate,
to allow us passage into our new home, which was once entirely

theirs, and theirs alone? And I knew that if these people under the bridge had been asked to whom the land belonged, some might have said, "The land." Who else? Who else could land belong to, but to land itself?

Bridges are not connectors, they do not join, they are simply ways to pass over—and what we pass over will come back to haunt us.

(Please follow the bridge, or pass over, until you arrive at *Translated from the Gibberish, Part Two*, on page 197.)

SWIMMING COACH

When Ulrich's brother told him that he should read a short story by an American named John Cheever, Ulrich immediately thought of better ways to spend the evening. He could gather the two- and five-rupee coins scattered in the corners of his room and go downstairs to the Irani restaurant and exchange them for paper currency. He could go to the laundromat across the street and collect his socks and underwear.

Or he could just stay put. Why do anything? His smallest movement would only add to the mayhem around him. Clare Road was a gaudy mix of hair salons, coffin makers, churches, cheap boutiques, and—worst of all—schools. Screaming brats had managed to hijack Clare Road, and now everyone and everything in the area had that unbearable quality most children possess.

"Just read the Cheever," said Moses. His brother was still looking for the key to his motorcycle. Ulrich knew, but did not say, that it was lying on the floor, at the foot of the table. "This guy, this loser American rich type, he's at a pool party, and he suddenly decides to swim all the way home through people's backyards."

"How the hell do you swim through a backyard?"

"Through their pools, yaar. He's tipsy and decides to go pool-hopping. But that's not what the story's *about* . . ."

"What do I care what it's about?"

"You're a swimmer, so I just thought . . ."

Moses had finally spotted his key. It was on a terrible key-chain for a motorcycle, one engraved with Moses's fiancée's name.

Ulrich pulled up his white T-shirt, revealing his round belly. "Do I look like a swimmer to you?" Ulrich slapped his belly; it felt hard. That was the strange thing about his belly: it looked like fat but felt like muscle. Today it was extra firm—he'd been constipated for two days. "I'm a coach, man," said Ulrich. "Very different from a swimmer. Swimmers swim, coaches sit and watch."

"Then just sit there for the rest of your life. Just sit there and stare out the window."

"Why does it bother you so much?"

"Because that's all you do. It's embarrassing."

"So is your fucking key chain."

Cussing always got to Moses. His brother had always been more polite than Ulrich, had been the darling pupil at school, whereas Ulrich's brain retained nothing; every line that he read passed through it, the way hot chai passes through a strainer. The only thing Ulrich excelled at was sport.

"I'll be back late," said Moses.

"So why are you telling me? I'm not your mother."

As soon as he said this, Ulrich regretted his words. Moses was trying to bridge the distance between the two of them with simple gestures; by asking Ulrich to read a story, he no doubt hoped the brothers would have something to talk about at night.

FROM THE VERANDA, ULRICH STARED out at Mongini's, the cake shop opposite. He envisioned his mother buying sponge cakes there. He could still see her, eight years after her death, wiping the edges of her mouth with her small white handkerchief, two dabs on the left and two dabs on the right. It was as if the white handkerchief and the dabbing had ensured that nothing cruel ever came out of her mouth. Unlike what came out of his own mouth.

Below, Ulrich could see Moses wiping the seat of his RX 100. Why did he wipe the seat five times? It was not a baby's bottom. It was a goddamn bike. Ulrich fought the urge to spit on it.

A year ago, he wouldn't have stopped himself. At thirty-nine, spitting would have made sense. But turning forty had changed things, forced a reckoning. He had lost almost all of his hair now, except for a meaningless tuft, an apologetic afterthought, at the back of his head, for which he still had to pay barbers' fees. And he was now a man with a moustache, a look he had always despised.

As he walked back into the living room, he spotted the book by John Cheever lying on the sofa. What the hell, he thought. Cheever's company in the bathroom might do his bowels some royal good.

ULRICH READ THE STORY THROUGH and through, but he did not know what to make of it. There was a distinct tempo to it, and each time he thought of closing the book, he found himself turning the page instead. His bowels were now empty, but his mind would not stop racing. For one thing, he could not understand why the man in the story, after completing a marathon swim through countless private pools (and a noisy public one), and even crossing a highway on foot, ended up standing outside his own home, which was locked, peering into it through a window, thinking his wife was waiting for him when the home was empty and deserted.

But the question that really burned him was this: What the fuck was Moses trying to tell him?

In the time since his brother had left, two hours ago, Ulrich had guzzled five beers. He was tipsy now, like Cheever's swimmer. A thought occurred to him: Had his brother finally learned to fight, to spit back? Suddenly, Ulrich circled the flat, a man on the verge of an important discovery. But when nothing came, and there was only the lazy grey of dusk to contend with, he had a sixth beer and went to sleep.

An hour later, he woke up with a start. He sprang out of bed with the liveliness of a sudden hard-on and rushed to the mirror. "I'm Ulrich!" he shouted at himself. That bastard is messing with me; I'll show him.

The name Ulrich, he knew well, was a distinctive one. Even in the Catholic community in Bombay—the Macs, as they were affectionately called—no one shared his name. His mother had named him after Saint Ulrich, and whenever he said his name out loud, as he had done just now, it seemed even more German than ever. Germans were tough. They did not shy away from confrontation. And Germany had his favourite football team. Its players had the precision of machines—machines that could produce sweat and were made of blood. As a swimmer, too, one had to be the perfect combination of human and machine. That had always been his belief.

Ulrich found he was perspiring, even though the ceiling fan was at full zoom. He took off his T-shirt and threw it on the bed, but this wasn't enough to cool him down. He took his shorts off too, and stood stark naked before the mirror. Then he put his Speedos on, stuffed some money in the side, and walked out the door.

On his way down the stairs, he passed his next-door neighbour, Sunita, who let out a shriek. Or maybe it was a squeal. Her husband was a scrawny man with toothpicks for legs. Clearly, Ulrich had done her a favour by showing off his muscular thighs.

With an air of confidence, he stepped into the street.

IT DID NOT MATTER THAT PEOPLE were staring at him. What did these morons know anyway? Cheever's swimmer had enjoyed the advantage of limpid pools and soft lawns and the occasional fancy drink to help him along his journey; he had not contended with the mocking stares of the Bombaywala. When a Bombaywala showed disapproval, you felt it in the very marrow of your being. Tonight, vowed Ulrich, he would use those waves of disapproval to build muscle.

The hot shoplights along the footpath made his dark skin shine as he took a left towards the fire station. Soon he was walking through Madanpura, a cocoon for the underworld and its contract killers and loan sharks. Yet Ulrich found the darkness of the streets soothing. If he were to walk here, dressed as he was, in broad daylight, he'd be sure to get a nice tight slap from someone. But now everyone was busy buying sweets or getting their beards shaved, and he strode along undisturbed. It was only near the Salvation Army that a lady in a burka gasped at him. He did not falter but hurried on towards the YMCA.

"I lost my keys," he said to the man at reception, and walked past him.

"But coach . . ." said the man, leaping up to follow him.

"Just chill, yaar," said Ulrich. "I'm doing only one lap."

"But . . . I thought you are here because you lost your keys."

"I lost them in the pool, man."

Ulrich dove in with perfect technique. When his large belly hit the water, it slid in smoothly, along with the rest of him, with minimum fuss. In his enthusiasm, he had forgotten to remove his rubber chappals and the money that was tucked into his Speedos. The chappals he let go after the first few strokes. They rose to the surface and stayed there, lolling about, as Ulrich reached the other end. Just like Cheever's swimmer, he refused to use the ladder to get out of the pool.

He remembered the fat kid whom he had trained that very morning, and how upset he'd been when the kid struggled to get out of the pool even *with* the use of the ladder. It was pathetic how this kid's pudgy arms had no strength; full of milk and butter and biscuits, his body did not deserve to be in the pool. "What will help my son?" the kid's mother asked Ulrich after the private training session.

"Iraq," Ulrich had wanted to reply, although he did not.

Now, dripping and sufficiently chlorinated, he coolly walked towards the exit near the canteen. The canteen owner nodded nonchalantly at first, but then, as he registered Ulrich's attire, his expression changed to one of bewilderment.

"What the hell are you doing?" he asked.

"I'm broke," said Ulrich. "Have to walk around in my chaddis. Tell the committee what a state I'm in."

Outside, stray dogs were tearing apart a piece of rotten meat the butcher had thrown their way. Ulrich spotted a taxi and slid into the back seat, despite the driver's protests.

"I'll give you seven hundred rupees," said Ulrich, thrusting his hand inside his Speedos and withdrawing a wet bundle of crumpled notes. "I want to go to Marine Drive, with two stops in between. That's all." Ulrich spread out all his money on the back seat, assuring the driver that none of the notes were torn. When the driver nodded, he handed him the cash. The driver put it in the glove compartment and took off.

A STALE WIND HIT ULRICH'S CHEST and sent a shiver through him, so he rolled up the windows even though the air inside the cab was hot. The first stop was a newly constructed building at Saat Rasta.

Ulrich got out of the car, walked up to the building's security guard, and told him to buzz Tony.

Tony was the only school friend Ulrich had kept over the years. He was now the creative director at one of the biggest ad agencies in the city. Ulrich disdained all the long-haired, goateed lunds Tony worked with. They walked around pretending they were geniuses, when all they'd ever done was come up with a byline for soap. It pissed Ulrich off, it really did. But it pissed him off even more that he did not have a single creative bone in his own body.

"Boss, what's wrong with you?" Tony asked, arriving at the security desk. "You smashed or what?"

"I need to use your pool."

"My pool?"

"Ya, men. It's urgent."

"The pool's closed," said Tony. "They had some issue . . ."

"Fuck," said Ulrich.

"Are you okay? Coming here in trunks and all . . ."

"All okay, men. All good. But I need a favour," said Ulrich.

"Sure, men," said Tony. "Anything."

"I need to swim at the Willingdon. Can you get me in?"

"Willingdon? No chance! Even *I'm* not a member. Those chaunts don't take any new members. Even if you have the cash."

The Royal Willingdon was the city's most elite sports club, with a pool surrounded by bougainvillea and coconut trees. Ulrich had only seen it up close once, when he'd applied for the job of swimming coach five years ago. He thought he had nailed the interview, until the hiring committee asked him to interact with the members' children. They wanted to see how effective he was as a coach. That's when he knew he was screwed. Not because he was a bad coach—far from it. He was a terrific coach. But that day from the pool he had looked up and caught the eye of a member who lived near the YMCA. This member had recognized Ulrich as the same sick man who had shown *Jaws* to a group of young boys at summer camp. Ulrich had told the boys that if they could watch *Jaws* and *then* get into the pool the very next instant, they would be able to swim anywhere, anytime. The kids had jumped with gusto into the pool immediately after the film—except for one. That boy had made an unnecessary fuss, and called his mother to take him home. No one at the YMCA had cared much about the incident; in fact, it had garnered Ulrich some accolades from old-timers who felt that kids nowadays had it too easy and needed some mental discipline. And even though Ulrich did a great job of interacting with his pretend students that day at the Willingdon, the member who'd recognized him had grinned and showed his teeth, and Ulrich had felt this old shark catching up with him, nibbling away at his ankles, and then his knees. And then came the final gash in the thigh, in the form of a polite "no" when he'd called the next day to ask if he had gotten the job.

"But why do you need to swim there *now*?" asked Tony.

"I have to," said Ulrich. "I just have to." Then he put his hand on Tony's shoulder, looked him straight in the eye, and said, "Will you help me?"

"I'll get you into another pool."

"No. It has to be the Willingdon."

"Why?"

"Because it's on the way."

"To where?"

Ulrich did not answer. He just mumbled that Tony was the best friend he'd ever had, and forced him into the taxi. On the way to the Willingdon, Ulrich slapped Tony's thigh. "What times we've had," he said wistfully. He adjusted himself in the back seat, and his wet, naked back made a squishy sound against the Rexine, like some small animal being squashed against the wall of a cage.

AT THE WILLINGDON, URICH ASKED the driver to wait in the parking lot. It was dark now, and he and Tony stayed close to the bushes as they approached the pool. It was impossible for anyone to enter the Willingdon through the main entrance without being seen, but the pool entrance was separate and the only obstacle was the man at the reception desk who handed out towels and placed your wristwatch in a drawer. Tony's job was to distract this man, which he did by telling him that a stray dog was running amok in the gentlemen's dressing room. This was easy to believe, because stray dogs did walk the lawns of the club from time to time, enjoying leftover sandwiches that patrons fed them from the leisure of their cane chairs.

As soon as Tony led the receptionist into the gents' change room, Ulrich entered the pool area through a white gate that resembled a pretty picket fence. He picked up a fresh towel, slung it around his shoulder, and scanned the pool. There were only three people in it: an old man who lay sprawled on the descending steps like some raja with his eyes to the heavens, his tummy partly outside the water, forming a half watermelon; a woman who was conscientiously doing laps, although her technique was all wrong—the way she stuck her head out of the water would surely lead to a neck injury at some point; and a teenager, his muscles rippling with stupidity.

Ulrich threw the towel aside and took a couple of deep breaths. He had arrived at the realm of the rich and successful, men and women who rang a small bell to summon a waiter and order Kejriwal on toast—which was just egg and cheese, but when these people ordered it, it had weight and taste—and when stray cats rubbed against their leather shoes, they threw scraps of food towards them, the same way life had thrown scraps of luck towards Ulrich, causing him to jump into the air for more, like a circus animal, only to bite into thin air.

But now, swimming at the Willingdon as if he were a member, as he was about to do, he would have the illusion of success, a temporary confidence and strength that would help him face these people as equals.

He expanded his chest and dove.

The first lap was purely functional, to get the arms and legs moving again, and adjust the body to the pool temperature, which was nice and warm. Once he had his breathing right, which occurred during the second lap, he felt as if he was on autopilot, and that was the trick, to conserve energy until, during the third lap, he forgot about energy completely, took his mind out of the equation the way yogis discard all thought during meditation but retain a simple and humble awareness.

The pool lights were on. They provided a gentle glow from beneath that reminded him of something—yes, of early mornings spent with his mother as dawn came, so softly, treating all humans like babies, all Earth creatures like fragile, magical beings who needed whispering and encouragement. But the water was too sharp, too chlorinated for him to keep his eyes open. He closed them, his body settling into an easy rhythm the way the heart settles during an afternoon siesta, that beautiful sinking feeling of falling *through* the mattress; even though he was on the surface of the water, in a sense he was going deeper, and he made a perfect turn when he hit the other end, his body curling into a fetus then gracefully springing to life, moving towards the other side with newborn energy. He was at home in the water, and it was from here that he would find ways to live, reasons to live. Suddenly he went deeper and cut across the pool, as though he had spotted an old acquaintance at a marketplace or among a crowd of strangers. No one could see him here, no human eyes could touch him, and he felt secure, un-judged, happy to pull in a modest salary and have enough money to buy the occasional pair of jeans or a round of drinks for a friend or two. Here, inside, it was warm and kind, and he came to the surface not because he needed air but because he had received something he could take along with him to his final stop. It was not what he had expected to receive; he had expected something electric, but he'd ended up imbibing a soft light instead, which was so much better. He stepped out of the pool, wrapped the towel around his waist, and left to find his cab. Tony would be okay to take a different taxi back home.

BACK INSIDE THE CAB, ULRICH ROLLED the window down. As the car took a left turn at Wilson College, Ulrich stuck out his chest and let the wind from the Arabian Sea bring him its salt. At Wilson, Ulrich had been one of the cool students, smoking joints, wearing jeans that he rubbed for hours with sandpaper to give the area near the thighs an almost-torn look. While others had studied history and literature, he gave drug-induced sermons on why "Comfortably Numb" by Pink Floyd was one of the greatest songs ever written, and how music could get you in an instant, it was the heroin of life, whereas books took their own sweet time and hardly gave you a lift, which was why, even though he was studying the arts, he refused to read. It was at one such free-falling campus lecture—delivered under a large banyan tree to about four or five regular stoners—that he managed to impress Angela, the hottest Catholic girl at college. He liked that she did not put any powder on her face to make her skin lighter. She had a dark radiance to her, an inner fuck-you shine that resonated with Ulrich. She was like Ulrich, he felt, but she had a brain. So one day, as she was talking to her friend, he picked up her copy of Chaucer, tore out a couple of pages, put some weed in them, and tried to smoke it. "It's useless," he said to her. "But if you and I smoke a large, healthy bugger and listen to Floyd, we'll be flying." Angela had liked his guts—although that came much later, about a year after she slapped him for wrecking her book.

Now, as the taxi took the stretch towards Marine Drive, Ulrich longed to be that age again, to smoke joints and bite Angie's dark, juicy, Christian thighs during long summer days and nights. But they were both forty now, and in different worlds. He was suddenly hungry for food; but in the next instant, the thought of eating repelled him. Perhaps he was nervous.

"Boss," he told the taxi driver as they approached a white building. "Just stop here." He looked at the taxi driver and smiled —the smile of a man who was thankful and defeated at the same time. The taxi driver nodded, let him out, and drove away. For a moment, Ulrich watched him go, imagining the notes in the glove compartment drying up and taking on the strange crispy shape of silver foil.

He climbed the steps to a ground-floor apartment and rang the bell. The door opened almost immediately.

"Angie . . ." he said, startled. "I . . ."

She looked as if she had put on some weight, and that made him perversely happy. She had also lost some juiciness; there was no doubt about it.

"Ulrich?" she said. "What are you . . . You know you can't come here."

"I know, I know. But I wanted to see you."

Angela seemed not to have noticed that Ulrich was wearing only a towel; she was clearly bothered by the very fact that he had shown up.

"How's . . ."

"She's not here," said Angela.

Ulrich felt relieved. It had been seven years, and even if his daughter were to stand before him this very instant, he might not know she was his. A baby can grow into anything; there are multiple permutations and combinations. The current man in Angela's life, the man who owned this expensive flat on Marine Drive, this man who was a Willingdon member, had once been Ulrich's friend. Angela had borrowed money from him for her dental work, without asking Ulrich, and this had hurt Ulrich deeply, so deeply that he had slapped Angie, and beat the shit out of his friend. This had been soon after his mother's death, a time when he was so raw that he eventually drove them into each other's arms. A slap had started his relationship and a slap had ended it. But perhaps Angie was not the person he'd thought she was. She had chosen money over love. Perhaps the reality of spending the rest of her life in one room, in a small flat on Clare Road that Ulrich shared with his brother, had been too much for her. The divorce had been swift and the deal sweet: the friend would not press assault charges if Ulrich gave Angie full custody of their daughter.

It was not the threat of criminal action that had scared him. Ulrich had signed his name in disgust on that sheet of paper because he knew he would never be able to provide for Angela and their child the way he wanted to. His signature was the clearest anyone could make, as clear as his self-loathing.

"I'm sorry," he said to Angela. "I shouldn't have come."

Here he was, apologizing once again. He saw how Angela leaned against the door, half her body shielded behind it, as if he were a common criminal. Slowly, she was closing the door, inch by inch, but just before she did, she looked into his eyes, and his body gave a tiny shiver. The sound of the door closing coincided with a stiff ocean breeze hitting the side of his neck and stomach. He suddenly felt very exposed.

He waited for the light on the corner to turn red, quickly crossed the road, and walked towards the huge black expanse of the Arabian Sea. He wrapped the towel around him like a shawl and stood on the sea wall. Below, large grey boulders were all that separated him from the water. During the monsoons, water levels rose so high the boulders were submerged and the waves lashed the shore relentlessly, until fissures appeared in the walls and made them crumble.

It was one big swimming pool out there, and if he swam in a straight line, he would reach the Gulf of Aden and enter Oman or Yemen, far away from Angela and his daughter, where he could earn much more money as a swimming coach. Around him, the promenade was littered with lovers, holding hands and cooing promises to each other in the same way he and Angie once had. He slowly lowered himself onto the boulders and, in doing so, lost his towel. It didn't matter. Paper cones were strewn across the boulders and a few plastic bags floated in the wind. To his right, the skyline of the city glittered, the lights in sky-scrapers burning passionately, the stars above less electric, less powerful. Tomorrow was Sunday—a working day for Ulrich. While the rest of the city read the morning papers, he would instruct a new batch of swimmers.

Perhaps, before going to work, he would wake Moses and tell him what he thought of the story. That Cheever's swimmer was not mad to look into his own house through a window. That he was looking at his past, trying to make sense of it, as all humans do, as Ulrich had just done. And perhaps Ulrich was luckier than the swimmer because Ulrich knew where Angela was. She wasn't his anymore, nor was his child, but at least he knew where they lived.

Perhaps Ulrich would also tell Moses the true ending of the story. How, long after Cheever's words ended, the swimmer walked around the perimeter of the house to the pool, to his very own pool, where the water was green and slimy, and slid in, without technique, without grace, just a body slipping into nature, the chlorine and algae and bacteria touching his skin, causing a chemical reaction, changing him, working on his brain, dissolving all its memories, one after another, the way acid does —moments shared with his wife and daughter turning into nothing, or perhaps returning to water, to nature itself, as nature had always intended, while the swimmer, always a mammal, shrank, collapsed, exhaled, inhaled, and sighed a final breath of relief as the world turned another day.

BEHIND THE MOON

Abdul was too tired to chase the rat. Perhaps the rat knew this, Abdul thought, because it wasn't trying to run from him. It moved slowly, inch by inch, along the base of the small refrigerator where Abdul kept his Cokes and Sprites. Whenever a customer left some liquid in the can, he would bring it to his tiny room at the back of the restaurant. At the end of the day, he would empty the cans into two separate one-litre bottles—Cokes in one, Sprites in the other. This reminded him of how he used to steal petrol from motorcycle tanks when he was young, sucking the fuel through a pipe until it burned the tip of his tongue, then letting it stream into a plastic bottle. But that seemed like a lifetime ago, his youth in Bombay. He had no use for petrol now. In Canada, he sat on a bus and stared out the window at what wasn't his nation.

The rat was really thin. It had now moved past the refrigerator, and towards Abdul's clothing rack. The one good coat Abdul possessed had been given to him by his owner upon Abdul's arrival in Vancouver five years ago. It had felt so soft and elegant at first, but had quickly revealed itself for what it truly was—a utilitarian shield against the rain and snow. It wasn't a piece of clothing; it was something you put on when you were under attack. And the grey woollen fibres that Abdul had put against his face on that first night in Vancouver, mistaking them for a welcoming touch, now seemed repellent. The rat was made of that same wool, in that same colour.

Abdul knew that if his owner saw him just staring at the rodent, not doing a damn thing about it, he would lose his mind. Qadir Bhai was kind as long as you did what he said. At this moment, his instructions would be: "Abdul, kill that bloody thing." And he would be right. A rat had no place in the Mughlai Moon. It was a place for lamb and kebabs. As a cook in the restaurant, how could Abdul allow the rat even a single breath? But Abdul couldn't kill it. That rat had found a way in but could not find a way out. That rat was him.

Abdul was a passport-less creature; he had used a tourist visa to enter Canada, and was now one of the invisibles. The food he cooked each day at the Mughlai Moon was the only sign of his existence, but that too disappeared—and rightly so, he felt —into the bellies of taxi drivers, construction workers, security guards, and janitors, reminding Abdul that he was digestible, someone the system chewed and shat out. He was no immigrant. His Indian passport was held by Qadir Bhai in an apartment with carpets and Netflix. His passport had better living conditions than he did. Qadir Bhai kept it for "safekeeping," alongside loads of cash that he never declared, cash made from Abdul's food, from Abdul's sweat. Once, the immigration authorities had come to the Mughlai Moon to quiz Qadir Bhai about Abdul's whereabouts, and Abdul had listened from a few feet away. He had been about to clear a customer's plate when he'd spotted the two men, sniffed out their air of authority. So he sat at the table and started eating from that same plate, chewing someone else's leftover chicken, pretending to be a customer. He had lost his hair, he had lost weight, he was no longer a twenty-five-year-old who bristled with energy, so there was little chance that he'd be recognized from his passport photo. With trembling limbs and tired eyes he sat there and watched as Qadir Bhai said, with the confidence of a seasoned actor, "That fellow is gone. He has run away. I brought him here to visit this beautiful city, as a favour to his parents. He has shamed me and my family. I had no idea he would do this." When the customer next to him got up to leave, Abdul skulked away too.

It unnerved him how easily Qadir Bhai could speak an untruth. Abdul's parents had been dead for a long time and Qadir Bhai had never even met them. When Qadir Bhai spoke those words, Abdul wanted to reveal himself to the authorities, clear his name and tell them that he had been tricked by Qadir Bhai, who had promised him he was "legal." But what good would that have done? Abdul would have been too terrified to speak in his broken English, using words that he had picked up here and there, scraps of a new language that had been thrown at him as though he were a beggar.

How he envied the men who ate his food; they had acquired Canadian accents, and when they ate his food with their bare hands, broke a piece of naan, and dipped it in their dal, their bruised knuckles showed, their calluses showed. These were honest calluses; Abdul had burns from stoves and frying pans and cooking oil—but his were not badges of honour, they were marks of shame and punishment. The men who ate his food held Canadian passports and strode through the streets freely, while he was forced to hide in a room at the back of a restaurant.

"If anyone asks, you live in someone's basement in Abbotsford," Qadir Bhai had told him. Then he'd handed Abdul a torn piece of paper: "Just memorize this address." Once, on Abdul's day off, he'd caught a bus to his fake address and seen how beautiful it was.

But everyone could smell a rat.

Especially in a restaurant, where the aroma of food was what drew people in. Which is why, perhaps, no one ever questioned him. One night, when the first *M* in the *Mughlai Moon* sign almost fell off and Abdul was sent outside to repair it, it occurred to him what his real address was.

I live behind the moon, he thought. And it made his tiny room feel a bit warmer.

TONIGHT, HIS BREATHING WAS GETTING heavier and heavier. It came over him every now and then, without warning—a sinking feeling, as if someone had taken dusk and poured it down his throat. Regret and anger, and a deep realization of his own impotence, brought him to his knees. Before he had come to this country, he fell to his knees only during namaz: his surrender to Allah had been glorious, so magnificent it had the scent of roses and the taste of sherbet. When he had prayed in Bombay, he got down on his knees out of sheer gratitude. Here, he was beaten into submission, a sick mareez looking to the sky for help. But there was no sky, just the cold grey paint of the ceiling. Everything was grey, everything was rat.

Abdul knew he had to snap out of this.

He walked over to where he kept his clothes. It was a shell of a cupboard, a hollow space without a door, a gift from Qadir

Bhai's university-educated son who had destroyed the cupboard in a fit of anger and then given it to Abdul as an act of charity. The empty hooks tacked to the upper panel reminded Abdul of the chickens that used to hang from hooks at the slaughterhouse in Bombay where he'd worked, where he'd taught his brother Hasan, fifteen years younger than him, how to skin the animals and cut through bone without making a mess. To think that he preferred the sight of dead animals to the grey woollen coat that hung here—as if a man was already in it, a very thin man, extremely still, afraid to move.

Behind the coat stood his cricket bat.

He grabbed the handle, felt the rubber grip against his palm. He hadn't thought of going for the rat, but the rat suddenly sizzled with energy and bolted off. Abdul didn't bother to trace its path. Instead, he felt the wooden surface of the bat. There were red marks on it, marks that he cherished because they were signs of victory, like the time his team had needed six runs off the final ball to win the league, and Abdul had pulled a shot out of nowhere—or so it seemed to the rest of the team—and won the match. Ten of his teammates holding their breath, then exhaling with joy. But things changed the minute he walked off the cricket field; the only reason anyone held their breath for him then was because he stank of the food he cooked.

His thoughts were getting the better of him tonight. Usually, these were winter thoughts, thoughts that came with rain. Tonight was dry, and winter was over. He told himself that all he had to do was get through the night. Tomorrow was Sunday, his day off. And tomorrow was the beginning of the cricket season.

He held the bat tighter, but all this did was make him sweat more, so he put it back in its place. He rolled out his mattress and switched off the light. In the dark, he imagined what being Canadian would feel like: to be able to sit at Tim Hortons and have a doughnut without feeling like a thief; to walk along the seawall in Stanley Park and not view the water as an endless extension of lost hopes and dreams; to be able to ride in a taxi once in a while; to afford an iPhone, to call Fido, as Qadir Bhai did, and give his full name and address and date of birth and make a *complaint*, or *demand* a better deal.

Someday, he thought. Someday.

His breathing calmed. He thought of that home in Abbotsford again, his fake address. How astonishing it would be to actually own something like it. It had a large wooden door with the number 123 on it. Outside, there was a lawn with a tree that was full in summer and went bald in winter. His breathing slowed even more. He walked up the three steps to the front door.

But that was as far as he could go.

Even in his dreams, he did not have the guts to enter his fake home.

THE NEXT MORNING, ABDUL SPRANG out of bed. The greyness of the night before was almost gone, and rays of the sun came in through his small window, a reminder that perhaps there was gentleness in store for him after all. He pressed the power button on his old Nokia cellphone—it took forever to come on—and saw that he had a text message from Randy, offering him a ride from Surrey to North Vancouver, where the cricket club was. He quickly gobbled down two boiled eggs and waited for Randy to show up.

Randy was a south Indian businessman who had started out as a restaurateur. He was built like a wrestler—short, stocky, hard as hell—and he opened the batting with Abdul. With his muscular physique, Randy couldn't run fast between the wickets, but when he hit the ball, he hit it out of the ground, so there was no need to run. Together, Abdul and Randy had garnered the North Van Cricket Club some serious acclaim.

"Mr. Abdul," said Randy, opening the passenger-side door of his car. "Long time!"

Randy always called Abdul by a nickname. Sometimes it was Mr. Abdul, sometimes Abdul Bhai, or Abdul the Great, or Abdullah, but never Abdul. Abdul had never bothered to ask him why. He felt feted when Randy called his name, blessed with some grace that he didn't have in real life.

"How are you, man?" Randy asked.

"Me good," said Abdul in his halting English.

"*I'm* good, man. *I'm* good!"

Randy had taken it upon himself to be Abdul's English teacher. Randy's English was impeccable—in fact he spoke it better than most Canadian-borns, each word so clear that Abdul felt the English language acquired extra gravitas under Randy's tongue.

"*I'm* good," said Abdul. He wished Randy could tutor him in English throughout the year, but Randy was part of his life only for a few months, four to be precise. Come September, when cricket season was over, his teammates went back to their lives, and Abdul to his.

It felt so strange, so exhilaratingly strange, to sit in a car.

Randy had a Lexus GX 470, an SUV that made other cars look tiny, as though Randy was seated on a throne that moved stealthily, a silent turbo-powered crocodile. Abdul couldn't help but think of the contrast with Qadir Bhai's van, an old, decrepit vehicle that smelled of vegetables and goat and had grains of rice strewn on the mat. Qadir Bhai had an expensive car too, an Audi, but Abdul never sat in that. It was reserved for Qadir Bhai's family. "You are like a son to me," Qadir Bhai had once told Abdul in that same liar voice he had used for the immigration officers. But that son never got to sit in the Audi.

"Come on, for fuck's sake," muttered Randy.

The car ahead must have been going 100 km/h, but that wasn't fast enough for Randy. He could go faster, wanted to go faster, and Abdul understood. One hundred wasn't enough for Abdul either—at least, not on the cricket field. While very few batsmen could even dream of scoring a hundred runs in the league that Abdul played in, Abdul was always hungry for more.

"You know, Al Pacino has this same car," said Randy.

"Oh."

"You do know who Pacino is, right?"

"Scarface," said Abdul.

"Right on," said Randy. He turned on some music—it was techno, and it made Abdul feel as if they were in space.

They sped through the highway that led to North Van, and Abdul, as always, marvelled at the stretch of tall trees that lined either side of the road. The air was so crisp here, and he immediately thought of the contrast with India's highways, long, dusty stretches of death, where transport trucks bullied every other vehicle, and accidents were so common they were cleaned up like the day's garbage.

"So . . . how're things at the restaurant?" asked Randy.

"Fine, fine . . . all good."

"Any new specialties from Master Abdul?"

"Nothing new," said Abdul. "Same mutton, same chicken."

"As long as it tastes good, right?"

"Right . . ."

Randy lowered the volume on the music. The techno played on, but now it seemed to come from very far away.

"Listen, Abdul, I want to talk to you about something."

Abdul felt a small shock. This was the first time Randy had called him by his name.

"I'm opening an Indian restaurant downtown. And I'm wondering if you'd like to come work for me," said Randy. "What's your PR status like? Did it come through?"

"Nothing come through . . ." said Abdul.

"But have you applied for it?"

"I don't know . . ."

That was the issue. Abdul had no idea what was going on with his status. All he knew was that his passport was sitting in Qadir Bhai's home, and each time Abdul asked Qadir Bhai what was happening, Qadir Bhai would say, "Abdul, my son, immigration laws have changed." Then he was told how complex the laws were, how nuanced, as Qadir Bhai twisted his hands this way and that, reminding Abdul of serpents.

"If you come work for me, my lawyer will handle things," said Randy. "I'll make sure you're able to work in my restaurant as a chef. Legally. I'll pay you well and you'll get your Canadian residency, no strings attached. If you want, you can walk out of my place the day you get it."

Abdul was taken aback. Randy had eaten at the Moon a few times, and had mentioned how much he liked the food, but this was a surprise. Randy had an array of chefs who worked for him. Abdul was merely a cook. But now Randy had called him a chef.

"Are you gonna say something or what?"

"But Qadir Bhai . . . he . . ."

"Let me take care of Qadir Bhai," said Randy. "All I need is a yes from you."

"I . . ."

"Take the rest of the week to think it over. But I'll need an answer by next Sunday."

Abdul nodded, dazed. This was a total googly.

If Qadir Bhai got a whiff of this conversation, he would fly into a rage. What if he threw Abdul out? What if he destroyed Abdul's passport? Qadir Bhai was the kind of man who demanded loyalty. And if it weren't for Qadir Bhai, Abdul's brother wouldn't be able to attend school in Bombay. Hasan's fees were taken care of, his books were taken care of, his uniform, everything. In a year, Hasan would write his tenth-grade finals and be ready for college. Abdul did not want to jeopardize that. It was the one promise Qadir Bhai had kept. Five years ago, when he had visited the slaughterhouse in Bombay and had spoken to Abdul's employer, Ali Bhai—Qadir Bhai's friend from the old days—he'd placed his hand on the Quran and said, "I will make Abdul a Canadian citizen. But it will take time." It had taken too much time, Abdul knew, but the other promise, the one about Hasan, had been kept, in its entirety.

Randy took the turn towards Norgate Park, past an Iranian grocery store where a woman was stacking up watermelons, and parked the car behind the clubhouse. He took his cricket gear out of the trunk. Abdul had only his bat with him, and a ball guard—everything else he borrowed from his teammates, and they were more than happy to lend him whatever he wanted, because he was their ace. The team even chipped in and paid his club fees.

If only his brother could see how beautiful the ground was. Abdul took the air deep into his lungs. It tasted great. How much better it would taste, he thought, when it was finally his.

He scanned the ground and remembered the places he had hit the ball last season. Once he had almost hit the nearby Indian reserve totem pole but was glad he hadn't. He didn't want to offend anyone. He looked towards the trees in the distance where balls had left dents in the trunks. Then something caught his eye. Something that hadn't been there before. He could hardly believe it. Through the trees, he saw the white marble minaret of a mosque. A year ago, it had been a church.

"When they build?" he asked Randy.

"Build what?"

"That," he said, pointing to the mosque.

"Oh. They started after the cricket season was over. Came up pretty quick, didn't it?"

Like magic, thought Abdul. He felt elated.

There were other mosques in the city, but he'd never felt like going to any of them. He missed his mosque in Dongri—it was the only one he had ever attended—the same mosque where his father had taught him how to pray. The very first time, when he'd watched his father close his eyes, he'd felt a calm come over him, as though his father, by closing his eyes to this world, was opening them up to another. Then, years later, it was Abdul who held Hasan's hand and took his brother on his first visit to the mosque. Two boys without parents, kneeling together; two boys who knew all they had was each other. When Hasan asked Abdul why they had to pray, Abdul replied, "To give thanks to Allah."

"But Allah took Abba and Ammi-jaan away," said Hasan.

"But He left me for you," said Abdul. "And you for me. So we give thanks."

At night, the singers would come and send their voices into the air, proof of their love and longing for the divine. Each time they sang "Dongri ke Sultan," Abdul was convinced that song was prayer too. The songs went into the air, circled around the minarets, rested on the domes, then continued upward, towards Allah, and at night showed themselves to the faithful in the form of stars.

Perhaps this mosque in North Vancouver was a star, too, and the fact that it was right next to the cricket field made it shine all the brighter. Maybe Abdul's begging and kneeling at the back of the restaurant had reached Allah, and Allah had sent a sign. Perhaps it had been here all along, waiting for Abdul.

Just like Randy's job offer.

Qadir Bhai, a man who shared the same faith as Abdul, had let him down.

And here was Randy, a South Indian—a Hindu—lending a helping hand, offering to make him visible. That made Randy more Muslim than Qadir Bhai.

Only one who behaved truly was a true Muslim. One who kept his promise. Why should Abdul be loyal to someone who had betrayed him? Someone who had used his passport as leverage? Who had made promises in India and pretended they did not count in Canada?

Qadir Bhai had another restaurant in Calgary, another Mughlai Moon, and when Abdul asked him who worked there, he evaded the question. But the answer had slipped out of his son's mouth one night, when he had woken Abdul up and demanded some dinner for himself and his drunken friends. There was another "Abdul type" in Calgary, Qadir Bhai's son had said to his buddies, another Bombay boy. Was this other Abdul hiding at the back of the moon as well? Was this how Qadir Bhai had bought his Audi?

Abdul looked at the cricket field. The grass was green, the colour of Islam. Another sign, another show of strength. He bent down and felt it against his palm, remembering the afternoon, on a chance visit to Stanley Park, when he had discovered that cricket was played in Canada. The soft carpet of grass had been a revelation. Unlike the dusty maidaans of Bombay, which sent him home with cuts and bruises, the grass was a homely rug—gentle and inviting. He had literally gone to sleep on it, feeling it against his back. He had been in Vancouver for more than a year by then, but this was the first time he had smiled. And the grass had smiled too. No one in Vancouver had smiled at him, but the grass did.

Now, as Abdul looked at Randy, he saw a person smiling, too.

BY THE TIME ABDUL GOT OUT to bat, the clubhouse was packed. The first game of the season always brought the immigrants and their families out of hibernation, and they drank beer and cooked burgers and smoked cigarettes while Abdul hammered the bowlers around.

Abdul always played under a fake name. Ever since the British Columbia Mainland League had started uploading the scores online, Abdul did not want to take any chances about being discovered. Not that the immigration authorities had the time to monitor cricket websites, but you never knew. Today he

was Manny, short for Manpreet. The real Manny was on a min-
ing contract in Calgary, and when he returned, Abdul would
use another player's name. Over the years, the opposition had
discovered this ruse, but they didn't care—it was an unspoken
rule that one immigrant would never tell on another. They understood each other's pain all too well.

Today, Abdul and Randy batted effortlessly. Both the opening bowlers, although fast, were ineffective against them.

"We make good partners," said Randy. "See?"

There was no doubt about it. They were creaming the bowlers, and the captain of the bowling side had become frustrated.
He made comments about how Randy only had one shot to offer,
a cross-batted swing, and that if it weren't for Randy's advanced
age, his own team would have felt free to bowl much faster—
anything to piss Randy off, and it was working. Abdul could see
that Randy was turning red and would burst any second.

"Hey, Randy," the captain said. "How come you're so fat?"

"Because each time I bonk your wife, she feeds me a biscuit,"
Randy replied.

All hell broke loose. The captain abused Randy; Randy refused to back down, and the umpires had to intervene.

"That prick," said Randy.

"No worry," said Abdul. "I show him."

Sure enough, the next over, the captain decided to bowl, to
try his hand at getting Randy and Abdul out.

"I'll tell you what," Randy told Abdul. "If you hit this guy
out of the ground, I'll give you a raise."

"I don't know my salary yet," laughed Abdul. "So how I
know if raise?"

"Just humiliate him. Make him long for his mommy."

"I do for you, man," said Abdul. He looked at the mosque, closed his eyes, and said a quick prayer.

When the next ball came at him, Abdul stepped out of his crease and lofted it high into the air. It took off into the stratosphere. He watched as it cleared the net that had been placed across one end of the grounds. The city had received complaints about cricket balls landing on the roofs of the homes that lined that end, so the club had put up the net, fifty feet high, across that side of the field.

No one had cleared the net before, and every player on the field stood still, following Abdul's ball as it soared over the net. Abdul allowed himself a brief smile, which vanished when he heard someone scream. It was an elderly woman working in her garden behind one of the homes.

"Shit!" said Abdul.

He bolted across the field towards the woman, Randy close behind. It took them a couple of minutes to go around the netting. When they reached the garden, the woman was holding the ball in her hand. Abdul was relieved to see that she wasn't hurt. But she was angry.

"What is wrong with you people?" she shouted.

"I . . . I so sorry . . ." said Abdul.

"This could have killed me!" the woman said. She was pressing the ball in an effort to demonstrate how rock-hard it was, but she didn't need to. Abdul knew. And he suddenly understood that she wasn't angry; she was terrified. If that ball had hit her head, it would have been the end for her. She was shaking as some of the players from the fielding team gathered behind him, intending to make sure she was okay. But the woman became more and more uncomfortable, and Abdul saw what she was seeing: all these men, bald men, hairy men, men with goatees and spiky hair, descending upon her garden, casting a shadow on her flowers, and the men were all brown and she was white.

Abdul turned to Randy and the others.

"She scared . . ." he said. "You go, please . . . I speak."

"We need that ball," whispered the captain. "Make sure you get the ball back."

"This is too much!" the woman said, her voice quavering. "Every summer!"

"I . . . my mistake . . ." Abdul said. The woman was panting now, and so was he—he had run all the way to her garden, and he too was pumped with fear.

Just as he was about to apologize further, the front door opened and a boy of about fourteen stood before him. Abdul felt relief. He could apologize to the boy instead of scaring this elderly woman even more.

"Buddy," he said as he walked towards the boy. "I so sorry, I hit ball in garden . . ."

"Don't go near him," said the woman sharply.

"Is okay . . ." said Abdul. "I just say sorry."

But as soon as he was a couple of feet from the boy, the boy began to scream and hit his head against the front door. Abdul became extremely aware of his cricket gear; here he was wearing cricket pads and gloves, and he had a bat in his hand. Was the bat scaring the kid? He backed away and began retracing his steps. The woman had moved towards the boy and was trying to calm him down.

By the time Abdul got back to the field, some of the players were lying on the grass, seemingly unperturbed by what had just happened. Perhaps nothing had happened, Abdul told himself.

But if nothing had happened, why were his nerves so jangled? His cricket gear suddenly felt so heavy. He needed a glass of water, some sugar perhaps.

"Did you get the ball?" asked Randy.

Abdul had forgotten the ball. Or maybe he hadn't. He imagined the ball landing on the woman's head, cracking her skull, and her lying there on the soft green grass, or on a bed of yellow flowers and dark-red blood. The sun beat down on him, and he felt dizzy. As he walked towards the clubhouse, the smoke from the barbecue grill entered his nostrils, making him even more lightheaded.

"Great shot, Abdul," said someone. "That was a monster six!"

He shook his head, and wondered if anyone could see that his hands were shaking too.

THE NEXT DAY, ABDUL WAS WOKEN from sleep by a loud banging on the door. He had been dreaming about the boy in the garden, and for a moment he thought it was this boy who was banging his head on the door. But it was Qadir Bhai. Abdul had overslept.

Without eating breakfast, Abdul got to work. To appease Qadir Bhai, he cooked a new dish—a dish he had promised himself he would never cook for Qadir Bhai because it was one his own father used to make for him. But now he wanted to start his week with something lovely, something kind, so he made egg bhurji with mutton. Qadir Bhai loved the concoction so much, he asked Abdul to serve it in the restaurant.

The next day, instead of allowing Abdul to bask in the glory of this new offering, Qadir Bhai accepted the compliments of the customers with a gracious nod, as though he had been finessing the bhurji for months and had finally perfected it. Abdul saw Qadir Bhai's bloated ego, his good mood, and decided to ask his question.

"Qadir Bhai," he said. "Just wondering if there is any news on my visa."

"You know how it is," Qadir Bhai replied. Then he lowered his head and spoke softly in Hindi. The two of them always conversed in Hindi—especially Qadir Bhai when delivering bad news and lies. "You'll have to wait for a few more months."

"But it's been so long," said Abdul. "Five years."

"I know," said Qadir Bhai. "I have to find a new lawyer, you see. My lawyer passed away—he was my friend, a fellow Muslim, who had offered to do this job for free, but his son is not cut from the same cloth. His son wants his full fee. Five thousand dollars."

"Five thousand?"

"What can I say? These young people have no souls . . ."

Perhaps you are talking about your own son, thought Abdul. How badly he wanted to say it aloud.

"Give me one more year," said Qadir Bhai. "I will sort things out."

"If you give me a loan, I will work my way through it, I swear. Please, Qadir Bhai. I just want to be legal here. I want to go back to Bombay, meet my brother, and come back here. As resident of Canada, not as a thief. I feel like a thief. Pay the lawyer and I will work off the debt. Please!"

"Where will I get the money from? The restaurant is not doing well. And whatever money I earn, some of it I send for your brother's education. And I pay you as well . . ."

"You pay me minimum wage," said Abdul. "Sometimes less."

"Abdul, times are tough. Please have faith in Allah. If Allah wills it, it will happen."

Perhaps Allah wants you to sell your Audi. Perhaps Allah wants you to stop giving cash to that worthless son of yours. Perhaps Allah wants you to keep your word.

Abdul said none of this, but he did not back down. He stood there in silence, hoping to make Qadir Bhai uncomfortable for bringing Allah into this. But instead, Qadir Bhai leaned on Allah even more.

"Allah will find a way," he said.

Yes, thought Abdul. Allah will find a way. Perhaps he already has.

That night, as he lay in bed, the light of his cellphone was the only thing that shone in his tiny room. It shone with hope, with two simple words emitting fluorescence that could have lit a stadium.

I in, he wrote to Randy.

He stared at the screen for a long time. Then he pressed Send.

When Sunday came, and Abdul and Randy were batting again, Abdul could barely contain his joy. On the way to the ground Randy had called his lawyer on the speakerphone, and this lawyer had sounded experienced and professional, not a bullshit smooth talker like Qadir Bhai.

"You're batting differently today," said Randy, between overs.

He was right. Abdul had no need to hit the ball hard. His timing was superb, he had a silken touch. He wanted to tell Randy it was all thanks to him. He could breathe now, he was more relaxed. Even his hamstrings, which were always tight from standing for long hours at work, weren't as taut. They were like the strings of a musical instrument. If you ran your fingers along them, sweetness would be heard.

A bowler, about to come in and bowl a fast one at Abdul, had stopped halfway through his run up, and was staring at something behind Abdul. When Abdul turned to look, he saw two cops walking towards the cricket pitch. One man, one woman.

The elderly lady from the week before stood near the cop car.

With each step the cops took, the grass became more still and quiet.

"Excuse me," said the male cop to Abdul. "Are you the gentleman who hit the ball into that lady's garden?"

Abdul struggled to speak; he knew a simple yes would do, but there was a lump in his throat. Nothing came out.

Randy came to his rescue. "Yes, officer," he said. "It was a mistake."

"Please step back," said the female officer. As she said this, she held her arm out, and Randy stopped in his tracks. Abdul felt cold; he began to shake.

"I'm asking you," said the male officer to Abdul. "Was it you?"

Abdul nodded.

"What's your name?"

This was the hardest question he had ever been asked. Last week he had been Manny, but Manny was back from Calgary. This week he was Harry, for Harpreet. But he wasn't Harry, either.

"Sir, I asked you a question," said the cop.

"I . . . sorry," said Abdul. "It went by mistake. Over net . . ."

"I asked you your name."

"My name . . . my name Abdul," he said.

"Abdul what? What's your full name?"

"Abdul Siddiqui."

"Did you threaten that lady's grandson?"

"Yes," said Abdul. "I sorry . . ."

"You *did* threaten him?"

"Officer," said Randy. "He's misunderstood. His English isn't—"

"Please stand back," said the female officer.

"I no say anything," said Abdul. "I only sorry!"

"Calm down," said the officer. "Did you raise your bat towards him?"

"No," said Abdul. "I bat in hand."

"Why did you carry your bat all the way to her home?"

"My bat in hand," he repeated. "My bat in hand!" He tried to calm himself down, but he felt as if he was sinking.

"That boy had to get stitches in his head," said the cop.

"But *he* bang on door. He crazy!"

"Excuse me?"

"I no mean . . ."

"Can I have some ID?" asked the cop.

"No ID," said Abdul. "ID home. I play cricket . . ."

"So you don't have ID? Where do you live?"

Abdul thought of the fake home with the large door, and the tree that was full in summer and bald in winter.

"Surrey," he said, and rattled off Qadir Bhai's home address. What else could he do? A fake address would be the worst thing at this point.

"How long have you been in Canada?" asked the cop.

"One month," said Abdul.

"Where are you from?"

"Mumbai," said Abdul. "I visiting uncle in Surrey. I go back India next week."

"So you're visiting?"

"Yes," said Abdul. A hundred thoughts ran through his mind. He imagined himself being handcuffed and taken away in the back of the cop car. He had seen this done in the movies; he had seen it happening in Surrey as well, to some of the very people who ate at the Moon.

"Where do you work?" asked the female officer.

"In restaurant," replied Abdul.

The minute he said this, he knew he was gone. He could feel the colour drain from his face. He had been tricked. He had made the blunder of his life.

"So you work here?" she asked.

"No, no," he said. "In Mumbai. I cook."

"I see."

"Sir, you'd better come with us," said the male cop. "Just for some questioning."

"But I no do anything," protested Abdul.

"This way," said the male cop. And Abdul knew it was best for him to do as asked. He had been a goner the moment the cops stepped onto the field. Whom did he think he was fooling? No one would come to his rescue. Qadir Bhai would simply deny everything.

When Abdul glanced at Randy, he saw the disappointment in Randy's eyes.

"I being kept here," he said softly. "I forced to work."

He could no longer look at Randy. He felt his own shame dripping down his face onto the grass, making it wet and heavy.

He started walking towards the cop car. The old woman was nowhere to be seen. She was a vindictive piece of shit, he thought wearily. He had done nothing wrong.

"I need help," he told the male cop. "I want to go back India. Please help."

But the cops were silent as they walked beside him. When Abdul reached the edge of the grass, he bent down and took his cricket pads off. Then his gloves. But he held on to his bat for a moment. Then, a second later, he accepted that even the bat was of no use. It needed to be shed. He left it on the ground.

He wasn't shaking anymore, but he felt a strange chattering in his mouth. It was his teeth, chattering at enormous speed. He felt himself gnawing at something; it was a strange feeling, but altogether familiar as well. As he sat in the back of the cop car, he felt smaller and smaller, greyer and greyer. His brown skin was turning into grey wool. He felt strong. He felt he could eat through metal, through Qadir Bhai's Audi. Then he felt the taste of hard paper in his mouth. He could feel Qadir Bhai's passport between his teeth, a Canadian delicacy that he was nibbling on, much hotter than the coffee at Tim Hortons, more mouth-watering than any deal Fido could offer. He nibbled at it with great relief, then spoke to the cops who were listening so beautifully, more than any white person had ever listened to him, and he could feel the passport turning into a different shape, the edges tearing, as though the outline of a new country was being formed, a country for traitors like Qadir Bhai, where rats like Abdul were in charge, ensuring that promises made were promises kept, and that when dreams were offered to people, a thousand rats would start singing, nibbling, gnawing in warning, and shame would drip down the jowls of men like Qadir Bhai, just as Abdul's shame had seeped into a country that could have been his.

CIRCUS WEDDING

Raju had written down the names of the people most likely to be responsible, in the event of his death. There was Arjun the elephant trainer, Tariq the trapezist, Mohan Drummer, and Mr. Patil, who was already dead, although that did not deter Raju from listing him. Raju could not afford a bank lock-box, or any such luxury, so he had decided to hand this list to the one person he trusted: his friend Ghulam Ali, the ice-gola man.

He made this decision in the mid-afternoon, when Ghulam Ali was at his busiest, but Raju did not care. He was determined to hand these names to his friend immediately. These were ominous times. When he had woken up that morning in his tent, he'd felt a shiver in his tailbone. He had last experienced a similar feeling two years ago, and later that day an acrobat had fallen and fractured his skull. The sound was unforgettable—crunchy but rock-solid. He cringed at the memory as he joined Ghulam Ali outside the gates of Johnny's Circus.

Ghulam Ali never smiled, except when he was making his delicious ice-golas. With his giant palm he would crush bits of ice against a thin stick and pour colourful syrup all over it: so red it looked like blood, so green it put grass to shame, so blue a thousand ink bottles could never match its depth. How he perfected these colours was his secret, and it had made him the most sought-after gola man in all of Byculla. For the past three months, ever since the circus had set up on the school grounds, Ghulam Ali's handcart had been surrounded by hordes of people —children, old men, women in burkas, handcart pullers, all seeking relief from the heat. A cheap remedy of coloured syrup and ice, that's all it took to soothe tongues and bodies.

But fame was not what motivated Ghulam Ali. His delight came from watching children slurp and bite with complete abandon. As soon as the children were gone, the smile vanished from his face and he took on the grimness of a security guard.

"Joker Babu," he greeted Raju. "Want one?"

"No," said Raju.

He hated being called a joker. He was a clown. Jokers were dumb duplicates, the equivalent of "Made in China" electronics, trying-to-be clowns who had no self-respect. They lacked inner sadness.

"Are you sure?" Ghulam Ali asked. "The sun is making a tomato of your face. This will cool you down."

"Not today," said Raju. "Not today."

Instead, he offered Ghulam Ali his sheet of paper. But the moment Ghulam Ali reached out to take it, Raju pulled the paper away.

"Wipe your hands first," he said. "They're wet."

Ghulam Ali brushed his hands against his blue trousers. He dressed in a Western manner—pants and a white vest. In winter, the vest would be replaced by a white shirt. Rarely was he seen in anything else. Of course, there was also the skullcap that he always wore, a sign of his devotion to Allah—although, he would always clarify, he was not a fanatic.

His hands dry, Ghulam Ali took the sheet from Raju.

The difference in height between the two men was comical. Ali was a giant and Raju far from tall. In fact, he was a midget —but call him that and he would erupt into a spitting, frothing ball. "Amongst small people, I am the tallest," he would say.

Ghulam Ali squinted to read Raju's handwriting. His friend's Hindi was almost illegible, but Ghulam Ali had practice: he had read all the love letters Raju had written to Sheila, the young woman who performed in Arjun the elephant trainer's act.

May 11, 2016. 12.30 p.m. Byculla (Mumbai).

I, Raju of Johnny's Circus, feel threatened by the four people whose names I have written below. If I die, they all should be held responsible. In no particular order:

Arjun the elephant
Tariq the trapezist
Mohan Drummer
Mr. Patil

Regards, Raju Madan. Born August 17, a long time ago.

Ghulam Ali looked at Raju.

Raju was squinting in the sunlight, his lips stretched out into a long *eeeeeeeee*, exposing one chipped tooth and gums brown as puddle water thanks to an incessant stream of Shivaji beedies. "I want you to safekeep this," Raju said.

Ghulam Ali was used to Raju's shenanigans. Ever since Sheila had come into his life, Raju had lost his already precarious balance. He was unreasonable and always seemed drunk, even though he never touched liquor. And there was no point arguing with him. Once his mind was made up, he was cement.

"You've called Arjun an elephant," said Ghulam Ali. "You mean to say elephant *trainer*."

"He's just as fat, isn't he?" asked Raju. "And hasn't the idiot named his elephant Arjun as well?"

"And why does Mohan Drummer want you dead?"

"Every evening when he bangs the cymbals, he looks at me."

"And who is Mr. Patil?" asked Ghulam Ali, hurt that he did not know. He and Raju were best friends. He knew about Raju's chicken pox, his polio, his mother's death, everything—or so he had thought.

"He was my school principal," replied Raju. "But he's dead now."

"Dead? Then why is his name here?"

"He hated me," said Raju. "Look, will you keep this for me or not?"

Ghulam Ali nodded. He put the ridiculous piece of paper in his pocket. Two or three days later Raju would ask for it again, just to make sure it was not lost. Ghulam Ali kept up with Raju's eccentric behaviour because he knew that deep down the joker was honest. What he lacked in height, he made up for in integrity. Raju treated stray dogs and children with respect, and circus owners with disdain. Only lately had his wisdom been replaced with a rabid passion for Sheila, but that too would pass. Ghulam Ali thought Sheila was too showy for Raju, her hips too curved, her powder too heavy, as though she was trying to hide something. But Raju couldn't see any of that; in fact, these were the very things he liked about her. Raju would talk about Sheila's hips all day long. He would tell Ghulam Ali that she was a real star and that when she put powder on her face, she looked like a gori.

Ghulam Ali wanted to tell Raju that Sheila did not look like a foreigner at all; she was as dark as the shade under a tree. But who was he to break his friend's heart?

"I'm off to meet Sheila for a movie," said Raju. "How do I look?" He adjusted his red shirt, pulling the hem down as far as it would go.

He had probably gone to the costume man, reflected Ghulam Ali, and used the man's iron. The shirt looked so stiff it almost crackled when Raju moved.

"You look fine," said Ghulam Ali.

"Just fine?"

"Like a red rose," he replied, pointing to his friend's shirt.

In truth, the dark hue reminded Ghulam Ali of congealed blood, but he knew that would be of little help to Raju's ego.

"You look fine," he repeated.

Raju nodded. How he looked would hardly matter in the darkened cinema. During the interval, when he would buy Sheila ice cream, all eyes would be on her anyway. At first. Then the odd glances would start. But Raju would revel in the jealous stares of men, feel their envy on his skin like the gentle lather of soap, which made the wisecracks less hurtful.

He left Ghulam Ali with a bounce in his step—you could call it a limp if you liked, but he preferred to think of it as a bounce—and the love in his heart and the tingling in his loins made him feel as if he had never been sick a day in his life, as if no chicken pox or polio had ever claimed him. If he could only rent Sheila a small room somewhere, a room for him and her, she would leave the circus forever. This was what she had promised him when he'd told her of his plan, his dream, and that he was close to having enough money to make it more than just a dream. She'd caressed his hand then, but it might as well have been his heart.

And when Raju took Sheila away from the circus at last, Tariq the trapezist, that gonorrhea-infested shit of a man, would never lay eyes on her again.

THE MOVIE WAS A DISASTER. Raju should have known better —matinees were always a mistake. A movie should be watched in darkness—darkness both inside and outside the cinema. But Raju knew that timing wasn't the real issue. Sheila had looked better than ever, and this made Raju sink into his own ugliness. The psychological descent had been rapid as he'd travelled in his mind from the cool air-conditioned seat of the theatre to the muggy floor of the small room he'd once shared with his mother in a Bombay slum. When other kids his age had gone to school, only too glad to escape the flies and river of sewage that trickled through the narrow lanes of their neighbourhood like some undesired gift from the rest of the city, Raju had wished to have bones so malleable he could curl into a ball and hide in his mother's lap until darkness came. She'd come to the corner of the room, where he shook and shivered in spite of the heat, and whisper to him, "Don't worry, you are loved. You are my son." But that only made him feel worse, made her kindness turn to nails, and when she combed his hair to get him ready for school, he always closed his eyes because he could not bear to see his own face in the mirror. His face was not deformed, but his state of being showed in his eyes—the terror of never being able to defend himself, or catch a bus, or run fast, or even walk without drawing attention—and his burden only became heavier when he found his father dead on the railway tracks after a drunken binge. Raju, at ten, held his father's head in his hands and called out for help, but the only response was a sideways glance from a man squatting on the tracks, releasing the previous night's meal. With his father gone, Raju had become the man of the house. And what a man he turned out to be—falling short on all counts.

"Why are you in such a bad mood?" Sheila asked him after the movie.

"Let's get some chai," Raju said, ignoring her question.

They walked to a nearby hole in the wall. An old poster of Raju's favourite actor brought the only hint of colour to the place. Johnny Lever was Raju's role model because he was short, and when he delivered his comic monologues, he soared.

Raju sipped his tea and stared at Johnny.

"So are you going to tell me or not?" Sheila asked.

"Tell you what?"

"Why your face is like a donkey's arse."

"It's Tariq," he said, and bit his lip the moment he blurted the trapezist's name. When jealousy stirred within him, it took a long time to settle. Even his tea was tasting bitter.

"I thought we were not going to talk about him," Sheila said.

"We weren't. It's just that you mentioned the donkey's arse . . ."

"Why are you so obsessed with him? You do trust me, don't you? Why can't you just let it go?"

Let it go? Let it go? Let it go? He wanted to repeat her words endlessly so she could understand how ludicrous they were. Even Johnny's expression on the wall had turned sceptical. His right eyebrow arched an inch higher.

"Never mind," Raju said, and flicked a fly away from the rim of his glass. *Never mind* that he had once seen Sheila kissing that spandex-wearing freak and it had made his heart shatter into a thousand pieces. "I promise never to speak about Tariq again," he said. "If I can ask you one last question about him."

"Look, I've already told you, I don't love him. And I kissed him before you and I were together. So I've done nothing wrong."

"That's not what I want to ask. I want to know something of a more serious nature."

"Okay, fine."

"But I want you to think about your answer. Don't just say the first thing that comes into your mind."

"What's the question?"

"When Tariq wears that body-hugging spandex unitard of his, how does he manage to divide each ball so perfectly? I mean, neither an inch here nor there, each testicle in perfect harmony?"

This made Sheila laugh, and she looked at him in a way Raju had never seen before, as if from a new angle. Her eyelids crinkled, her lips spontaneously erupted like a pink flower trying to blow a kiss at a passerby, and now there was a scent in the air that made their little chai stall smell like a perfumery. Even the rat that scurried past Raju could not dampen his success. This, he knew, was why she loved him—he made her laugh. And he had laughed all the way into her bed, and he intended to stay there until he died. And if she died first, well, he would just lie on her body until it stank, and her putrid flesh became one with his. Of course, he would never tell her that because it was kind of extreme—but love does that to you, he told himself. Love had also made him spend no little part of his savings on a wedding ring. Each time he looked at the ring, it was not the shiny stone that caught his eye, but the hole that the finger would go through; when you bought a ring, you were simply buying a hole, an opening for a new wound. For a month he had stared into that hole and thought of returning it. But today, as Johnny in the poster looked over him, Raju realized that there was no such thing as the perfect day, the perfect moment. He would think of the hole as a hoop, and he would jump through it, into a new life.

He held Sheila's hand and walked out of the chai stall.

THAT EVENING, AS SHEILA got ready for the show, as she stared into her large mirror and powdered her face for the third time, Raju stood beside her, in costume, grinning at the thought of being married to her. When she bent down and adjusted his purple bow, he licked a drop of sweat off her neck, making her squeal.

When it was time for Sheila's entry, the band sent out a spectacular drum roll that rose above the crazy whirring and hum of the giant fans spread throughout the tent. Raju stood backstage and watched Arjun lower his trunk for Sheila. It was so loving and natural, like a tree branch moving towards a human being, offering comfort and support. Sheila lay on his trunk, sparkling and precious. Raju knew she was so much more than a showpiece; she could sing, she could dance. But the circus owners didn't want her to. She was Nepali, after all. Her oriental features meant some people looked down on her, thought of her as cheap, as flesh to be bought and sold at night after the circus lights went down.

As Arjun and three other elephants circled the circumference of the ring, close to the audience, the children started clapping and tried to touch elephant skin. Raju wanted children of his own someday, although he worried they would come out like him and stay small forever. This was not a fate he would wish upon any child, least of all his own, and he feared his guilt would course through him with greater intensity than the jealousy he felt when Sheila waved and winked at the crowd. Why did she have to wink? A queen simply waved. A wink gave people the wrong impression. He understood that she was a performer, it was all an act, but to have men breathe upon her, to feel their hunger and have a dirty film running through their minds . . . The wink could be avoided, in his opinion. But it didn't matter. A ring on her finger would give her respect, and would once and for all change the way people looked at her.

He slunk away from the bright lights and decided to warm up for his act with a few strong puffs of a beedi. He went in search of Ghulam Ali. Raju hated smoking alone. To him, one shared a beedi; it was a communal act, a communion with nature. The tobacco, the rough paper, the fire of the match, these were all elements of the Earth, and because he felt that way, he never coughed, his lungs were always clear.

"Ali," he said, offering a beedi to his friend. He always called Ali by his last name just as Ghulam Ali always called him Joker Babu. "I'm going to propose to her tonight."

"Oh," said Ghulam Ali.

"Oh?" Raju said. "Is that how you greet good news?"

"I'm surprised, that's all," said Ghulam Ali. He was speaking the truth, but he did not want to tell Raju exactly what kind of surprise he felt.

"You don't seem too happy about it," said Raju.

"No, no, it's just . . ."

"Why don't you like her?"

The honesty with which Raju asked that question made Ghulam Ali shrink even more from the truth. He could see that when Raju lit his beedi, his hands were shaking. Perhaps they were shaking with disappointment in his friend.

"I just don't want her to hurt you," said Ghulam Ali.

"I'm hurting anyway," said Raju. "When I am with her, I hurt because I feel I do not deserve her. When I am without her, I hurt because I long to be with her. Love is a screwed-up thing."

Ghulam Ali took a large dum, keeping the tobacco smoke inside him for longer than usual. Then he coughed out the truth. "I just hope she stays with you."

Raju understood what his friend meant. Anyone could see that he and Sheila were a mismatch. But was Raju doomed to spend his life only with someone his own size? Did the size of the heart not matter? Was the expanse of love he felt for Sheila not as wide and deep as any sea? She could feel that, she could sense it, which was why he could pleasure her during their lovemaking. All the love he had never received from his father, all the longing that he still had for his mother, all the rejection he'd faced as a child, all the taunts he continued to bear as an adult—all this he converted into something good when he kissed her. No other man, no matter how tall and strong, could give her that.

"She'll never leave me," said Raju. "I have a plan."

"A plan?"

"I'm going to get her pregnant. That will make her fat and large for a while. Then the next year she'll be breastfeeding, so she'll be busy. After that, I'll get her pregnant again. So the same cycle will repeat. Then I'll get her pregnant a third time. By then, there's a good chance she'll go into a depression. So she'll need me even more."

"That's . . . romantic."

"I'll do anything to keep her."

"Joker Babu, I hope you have not told her this."

"Just be happy for me, Ali. That's all I ask. Give her a chance. Give us a chance."

"Who is Ghulam Ali to not give love a chance?"

Perhaps, thought Ghulam Ali, he was being unkind about Sheila. After all, she had stayed with Raju for more than three months now; maybe she genuinely cared about him. Except that there was something about her, about her and Tariq, that Ghulam Ali did not trust. Whenever he saw Tariq on the trapeze, he was reminded of a long lizard, hanging upside down, its beady eyes scanning the entire tent from up above. It was a cold gaze, the way one felt when a fridge door suddenly opened and sent a warning through the body. He just hoped he was wrong.

THE BEEDI WAS BITTER, but life was sweet. There was a lilt in Raju's walk as he entered his tent. He still had a few minutes left before he was on. He went to his steel trunk and removed the red velvet pouch that he had placed at the bottom, underneath his clothes. When he drew open the strings of the pouch, he could feel a new life opening along with it. The ring tucked inside would help him fulfill his dreams of having a family. Everything that he had saved up so far, all the money earned from somersaults and slapstick stunts performed in front of an audience, was stored in this ring; hours spent perfecting falling through the cane web of a chair, then walking with the rim of the chair around his waist, seemingly unaware—that was the trick of the clown, to be an acrobat who was a total nincompoop, and to be a nincompoop, one had to feign a lack of awareness. While the acrobat concentrated on every move, the clown had to go one step further: he had to forget everything so that his actions looked natural. In this sense he, Raju, was far more gifted than Tariq, even if the local public did not understand his talent. But now, this no longer mattered—all that hard work had paid off, all that hard work rested in this ring. It was all Raju could afford, but his intention was pure. And that was why the ring sparkled so intensely. That and the special woman it sparkled for.

The day had started badly, with the list of names of those who were gunning for him, but tomorrow Raju would ask Ghulam Ali to return that note. He would tear it up, or even burn it. Or perhaps he would write a new note, listing the names of people who had given him life: his mother, Ghulam Ali, and now Sheila. Sheila had made his insides change; if a doctor were to cut him open this very second, he would be astounded to find, in the place of Raju's intestine, a long garland of marigolds and lilies, such was the hope flowering within. Raju put the velvet pouch in his pocket and went towards the tent. It was time.

He sat on a tricycle and rode it around the ring. Five red balloons were tied to the seat of the tricycle, and as he pedalled Raju made a mental note to tell the band that their tempo was too slow. Or was he speeding out of sheer excitement? He was in a hurry to get to the centre of the ring, but not before he made sure that Sheila was watching. He had told her earlier that he was trying out a new routine and wanted her opinion on it. As he got off the tricycle, he faced the audience. Behind him, the tricycle was rising in the air, the balloons helped by an invisible cable. This always got a laugh. In response to the laughter, Raju looked at his fly to see if it was undone, then smelled his under-arms to check for bad odours. Finally, he gave a shrug and turned around, then smacked his own head with his hand when he saw that the tricycle was missing, hitting himself so hard he knocked himself out. As he went through his routine, Raju felt great. He was timing his falls beautifully tonight.

Next, he took a piece of paper from his pocket. He checked his shirt for his reading glasses, but found a pair of dark glasses instead. He put these on, tried to read the note, then shouted: "Who turned the lights off?" Another round of laughter. Upon realizing his folly, he found his reading glasses. Throughout his routine Raju could feel the ring in his pocket, the pulse of a future life. At one point, as he roped in a little boy from the audience and included him in his routine, he noticed Sheila looking on, approvingly. There was no doubt he would be a good father. Boy or girl, he would welcome the child. As he tumbled through the air and fell expertly on his buttocks, he tried out names. He would call the girl Julie. The boy he would call Johnny, after Johnny Lever. Johnny and Julie. Why not have two? As his act ended, he signalled to the band, and they began to play Raju's favourite Hindi song: "Mere Sapno Ki Rani." It was an instrumental ver-sion, but Raju thought of how he had sung this song to Sheila a hundred times, calling her the ultimate Queen of his Dreams.

Now he looked over at Sheila and waved for her to walk out and join him. For a second, she seemed confused, but Raju pointed to the band, as if to say, "Can't you hear my love for you?" The spotlight hit her and she became a silver thing in silver light. Raju felt as if he was in a trance. He had never before seen a being such as Sheila. It was time to go down on one knee. But first, he put his hand in his pocket and removed the velvet pouch. It was Ghulam Ali who nudged Sheila forward. The audience was hushed, not sure if this was part of the act. But now the ringmaster took over, calling into the microphone that this was real, and that Raju the Clown was hooked, booked, and cooked, and the crowd went wild. They only fell silent again when they saw Raju, the tiny man, drop to one knee, opening himself up to love.

Sheila was only a few steps away from him now, and when he looked up at her, he saw she was smiling. Was there a tear in her eye as well? If only his mother was alive to witness this: five hundred people watching Raju propose to his wife. The same Raju who had wept in her lap every night because he could not make a single friend. His mother would love Sheila; yes, perhaps she might not approve of Sheila's short dress, but that was okay.

Still on one knee, he placed the ring on Sheila's finger and looked up at her face again, and as he did, he caught a glimpse of the trapeze hanging high above. It was still and empty.

THAT NIGHT, AFTER A HUNDRED congratulatory thumps on Raju's back from his fellow circus performers and audience members, Raju and Sheila lay next to each other in Raju's tent. On most nights, Raju felt uncomfortable lying alongside Sheila, but tonight, with both their heads on the pillow, the fact that his feet reached her knees did not dampen him.

"How many do you want?" he asked her.

"How many . . . ?"

"Children," he said softly, kissing her ear.

"Oh God," she said. "We're not even married."

"I'm serious," he told her.

"But Raju, if I get pregnant, how will we live? If I stop working . . ."

"Let me take care of that."

"But how? All the money you spent on this," she said, raising her finger, admiring the ring. "How much did this cost?"

"In the shop it cost too much," said Raju. "But on you, it costs nothing."

"I don't deserve this. I don't deserve you," she said softly, facing away from Raju.

"Just answer my question."

"Let's get married first," she replied. "Then we'll talk."

"I've booked the church for Sunday," he said.

He longed to have a church wedding. He did not care much for religious ceremonies or vows, but he liked the way the light fell through stained glass windows. That was all. The circus would come to an end on Saturday night and the next morning he and Sheila would get married. On Sunday evening the circus would move from the school grounds of Clare Road to the suburbs, where he would perform for another three months. This would give them both a decent amount of cash—nothing great, but enough to allow them movies and clothes from time to time, and late night auto rickshaw rides along Bandstand.

"This ring is loose," said Sheila. "See?"

She moved it back and forth on her finger, and the diamond turned as she did so, like a small planet showing its shiny face then moving away to grace another part of the universe. Raju clasped his hand around hers and held it to his chest. Nothing needed to be said. After a long time, luck was with him, or perhaps kindness. To have a kind person next to you, and just one hand to hold. He fell asleep, sinking into the blessed future of his own life.

SOMETHING WOKE HIM. It was the smell of elephant dung, unusually strong. He opened his eyes. Sheila wasn't next to him in bed. Through the fabric of the tent, he could see shapes, two human shapes. He recognized one of them: a tall, lanky male with long hair; maybe what he had smelled wasn't elephant dung at all but this male, whose rottenness was hidden by his beautiful physique. He heard Sheila's voice whisper hoarsely, "No."

Raju jumped out of bed and went outside. Only Sheila was there, scanning the ground for something.

"What's wrong?" he asked.

Sheila didn't answer, and wouldn't look at him.

"What's wrong?" he asked again.

"It fell," she said.

"What fell?"

"I can't find it. I went for a walk. It was on my finger . . . but now it's not there."

"Who was that here with you?" he asked.

"What do you mean?"

"Just now, there was a man . . ."

"There was no one," she said. "What are you talking about?"

"I saw . . ."

But Raju was no longer sure what he had seen. His thoughts were confused. Why had Sheila gone for a walk in the middle of the night? What had happened to the ring? He fell to his knees and started scanning the grass inch by inch.

"It's not there," Sheila cried.

"Why did you go for a walk?" He kept his head down, searching frantically, casting pebbles aside.

"I was so happy, I couldn't sleep. I thought of home . . . of my sister and mother . . . how happy they would be," she said.

"There was someone with you just now," Raju said. "I saw—"

"Will you stop?" she said. "Please stop."

Her voice cracked, and so did Raju's life. He was sure of what he had seen. He had seen shapes. And shapes could not be trusted. Weren't shapes illusions? Weren't shadows meant to scare people, to make things seem larger than they were? He could feel Sheila beside him, crying. Even though she hadn't made a sound, he could sense her going under, the way a beautiful cat hides under a chair when there is too much noise. He could not bear to look at her, so he stayed on his knees. He was walking on them now, quickly covering ground. Luckily for him, the outside lights were still on. He would scan every inch around the circus tent even if it made the skin on his knees raw, even if all he had found so far were bottle corks and chewing gum wrappers and a five-rupee coin, which he threw aside along with more pebbles and some worms. Was everyone in on it? Everyone on his list from yesterday morning, all the ones who wanted him gone? Had Tariq managed to seduce them all? Had Ghulam Ali joined them as well? No, no, that was unthinkable.

He remained on his knees, head down, kneeling before the earth, where he and the ring surely belonged—anything to prevent him from looking at the face of his beloved, where he knew exactly what he would find: more shapes, more shadows.

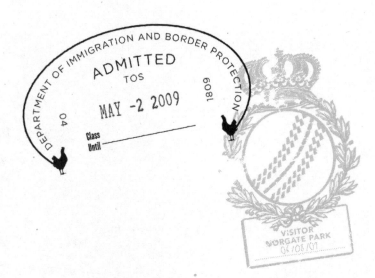

BUTTER CHICKEN

As a child, Sujoy had constantly heard that New York was just as crowded and dirty as Bombay. "More people," was what his father would say. "Who wants to see more people?" Then he would lower his head like a crow and, with bent beak, continue marking the papers of his geography students.

Now, decades later, here was Sujoy in New York: forty-five years old, seated in a chair opposite a talk show host, staring into the dark—or rather, into the bright lights and the darkness beyond—where the audience waited for him to speak. They were mostly women, he'd been told, and some had travelled a fair distance to attend—from Texas, from New Orleans, from Kansas, from places he remembered seeing on his father's maps. Those maps had been in the atlas, that precious atlas, which he was allowed to peruse only in his father's presence. He'd been fascinated by all the blue and green, marvellous as a magic trick, waiting for him to dive into. He was always extra careful when he turned the pages, following his father's strict instructions: with the tip of his forefinger Sujoy was made to unpeel the top right-hand corner of the page, bring it towards him like a giant wave, turn it, then let it fall gently. Sujoy wanted only to get to the next page so he could eat the blue and green all over again, but his father would hover above him, ensuring that some of the magic was lost. That was the true purpose of fatherhood—to kill magic. When Sujoy would look to his mother for support, she would only smile her gentle smile, weak as a muscle that had atrophied.

More people. That's what his father had seen in that atlas. No matter the country, state, or city Sujoy pointed to, what his father saw was a disappointing race of humans, sweaty and pointless, sweating pointlessly. Where Sujoy saw crystal-blue water, his father saw sweat, pools of it, rivers of it, oceans of it. As a child, Sujoy had tried not to inhabit his father's mind, but often he couldn't help himself.

Even now, in New York, he heard his father's voice: *More people.*

But today they were here for him—for his food, and to learn the art of making an "authentic" Indian meal. He was constantly told his food was "so authentic." At first he had not really understood what this meant. He cooked the only way he knew how, the way his mother had taught him. But after he had eaten at some Indian restaurants in New York, the meaning became clear. Some of the meals had been great—but that was like saying the music in an opera was superb, except for when the soprano hit the wrong notes.

The audience laughed when he said this, and the host gave him a warm smile. Sujoy liked her warmth. He had seen a few episodes of her show, and appreciated that she didn't cut her way into the lives of her guests with a scalpel. In any case, there was nothing sensational for him to tell about his past.

"No, no," he gushed, when she asked. "Nothing here . . ."

His story was nothing like that of the other people she had interviewed over the years—politicians, movie stars, artists, trailblazers. That was the word James had used: trailblazers. James, his business partner. James, who'd shared a flat with the host in university. They were great friends, and she was doing James a favour by interviewing Sujoy. When Sujoy had expressed his discomfort at being on the show through the back door, James was very clear: "If she didn't think you had something, she'd never take you on." Sujoy had done well during his mock interview over the phone. But now, this was for real. And reality, even when it came to the most mundane acts such as dusting furniture or filling out a form, always arrived with a degree of difficulty for Sujoy.

"Nothing here," he said again. The host stared at him for three seconds, maybe four, but it felt like hours.

"Butter chicken," she said at last to the audience. "We're here to learn how to cook Gupta's Butter Chicken."

At Sujoy's restaurant, this dish was named after him; he'd used his last name instead of his first because it had a better ring —or so he was told. But for some reason, when the host said it out loud today, the words startled him. There was nothing to be afraid of, he admonished himself. He could make this dish with his eyes closed. In fact, he felt it was imperative to close one's eyes at some point during the cooking, to get the aroma right. Just calm down, he told himself; that was for later. Nothing to worry about, Sujoy. This is the most common of Indian dishes, one that the goras love, especially the Brits. The whole country of England lived on butter chicken, didn't it? Sure, these were Americans —but they had embraced it too. It was the signature dish in his New York restaurant. That was James's doing. Sujoy knew nothing about selling, but James could sell skis to a Bedouin.

"Just go out there and be yourself," James had told Sujoy on their way to the studio.

This was code for "don't screw up." If the gig went well, it could lead to more restaurants. Sujoy had three of his own in Mumbai, and was now partner in the one in New York. Two of the greatest cities in the world, Sujoy thought, even though his father would strongly disagree. *More algae, more bacteria.*

As Sujoy moved from his chair opposite the host to a table piled with ingredients, he felt a shiver up his spine. A cold tingle of excitement about future prospects, about those women from Kansas and Texas going back home and making his butter chicken for their Johns and Jacks. "You'll be the next Colonel Sanders," James had said to him, half in jest. But Sujoy didn't want to be the Colonel; he just wanted to be major. He had re-hearsed this bad joke in his head, to use should the opportunity arise. He walked towards the table, which was so clean and sanitary he felt as though he was in a lab. He had a sudden, in-tense desire to mess things up. So he did.

"There," he said, when he was done. "Now it looks like my mother's kitchen."

OUTSIDE THE HOUSE IN BOMBAY, IT was especially hot—oven hot, fire hot, call-it-what-you-like hot. For the past couple of weeks Sujoy had begged his father to take him swimming, but the fees at the YMCA were steep, and the cheaper Sunday swims inconvenient for his father. Sunday was a day for rest, endless cups of tea, reading the morning papers, and talking about the Congress Party, about Indira Gandhi. Sunday, every Sunday, was when his father told him, "There is a difference of only one letter between *India* and *Indira*. That *r* stands for *respect*. She commands respect." Sunday was the day Sujoy's father assessed the state of the nation; for Sujoy, Sunday was the one day he got to leave his nation behind, at least in his imagination.

"Meena, you may fetch him the atlas," his father would say.

And Sujoy's mother would dutifully go to her husband's study, which was nothing more than a small nook in the wall, with a rickety desk and a bunch of ink refills. But on that desk, placed like a monument, was the atlas. Sujoy's mother would "fetch" it, as though her husband were unleashing a playful dog onto the grass. A cloth was placed on the floor, and the atlas on the cloth.

The Times Atlas of the World. A cover so generously blue, it was perfect for a hot summer's day. Its price, fifty-five pounds, a small fortune. Sometimes Sujoy tried to convert that into rupees, but the sum was so vast, he could never complete the calculation. Most important of all, at least to his father, was the symbol of a huge crown on the first page, with an inscription:

E R
To Her Majesty
Queen Elizabeth II
The Times Atlas of the World
Is with her most gracious permission
Respectfully dedicated by
Her Majesty's Cartographers
John Bartholomew & Son Limited

Sujoy's father was a huge admirer of the monarchy. While he gave his nod to Indira personally, he felt the Brits had bolstered

India, given it respectability and class, and proof of that lay in the debris that remained once they'd left. Garbage everywhere, flies, trains that smelled like sweat balloons, open-air pissing and shitting, corruption that could break your spirit in two and then slice it in half all over again. "What did we do with India?" His father didn't sing—at least Sujoy had never heard him do so —but when he lamented about India, he became a songbird, and this was his chorus. And when he touched his atlas, he traced his fingers along its pages as a blind person would, as if searching for something.

Sujoy's father had *won* the atlas. Sujoy vividly remembered the day this had happened, two years ago. It had been Sujoy's eighth birthday, a Sunday. He and his parents were listening intently to the radio because his father had entered a quiz show and the results were about to be declared. When the name of the winner was called out, his father's face had changed, registering a shock—but not the happy kind. At first, Sujoy had seen a light, feathery caress, as if made by an artist's brush, a stroke of joy that added a lucky hue to his father's face; but then, almost instantly, the face had changed, and happiness was replaced by a dawning realization: *What if this is the best thing that will ever happen to me? What if this is it?*

That's what his father's expression had said. And that became his father's Sunday face.

Now, every Sunday, Sujoy stared at that face. It had bothered him initially, but after a while he chose to accept the good that had come with the arrival of the atlas. Who needs the YMCA? Sujoy thought, when I can simply dive into these pages of oceans. He chose to focus his interest on the South Pacific Ocean, the Bellingshausen Sea specifically, near the northern part of

Antarctica, the part that looked like the continent was giving a thumbs-up sign to the rest of the world. Cold, shivery waters. Perfect for the Bombay heat, perfect for bringing his heart to a sudden freeze, the way love does.

"To think the Queen has laid eyes on this same atlas," his father often said. But that was of no consequence to Sujoy. "Geography and history are linked," his father would continue. "Yes, I teach geography, but geography isn't just land and water, shapes and sizes. Geography is made up of nations, and nations are shaped by history."

But what about this ocean's water? Sujoy wanted to ask. This ocean so cold, so daring in its loneliness. Yes, he felt that loneliness. This ocean had no fish, no boats, nothing. It was probably not aware of its own colour, its own temperature. It just lay there, deep and stately, the way Sujoy wished to be. Perhaps if he plunged into it, immersed himself in its iciness, he might be able to display some of its courage. Coldness was not aloofness; it was dignity, it was the ability to not *need*. Even though he was only ten when he thought this, he was already aware of his need for acceptance, for love, aware of the stupidity that was associated with the ideal of the family unit, with mother, father, and child; aware of the ridiculousness of the need to make friends and keep them. Why did one have to *keep* friends? They were made then unmade. At least, that's what his own experience told him.

"Look at this boy," his father said. "I'm explaining things to him and he's not even responding."

"But I was just . . ." Sujoy fell silent. Couldn't his father see the water, hear it call him, the way you opened the refrigerator in the dazzling heat and the ice felt so loving, nurturing, soothing?

"Papa, do you know the Bellingshausen Sea?" he asked.

His father was silent. He was using a pen refill to scribble lines on his palm. He did that absent-mindedly, to combat the eczema. Every now and then, especially in the heat, his palms would be covered by water pustules, and he would scratch them with his refill, and after the itch had abated, his palms were full of red and blue lines. It occurred to Sujoy that perhaps his father, a firm believer in palmistry, was trying to add lines to his palm, to rewrite his own destiny. Sujoy had so many questions for his father, but for now he would stay with the Bellingshausen Sea.

"Do you know it, Papa?"

"Why did you choose that sea?" his father asked.

"I didn't. It chose me."

"Look at this boy," said his father. "Why does he have to talk like that?"

His mother smiled, as she always did; it seemed to Sujoy that this was all she knew how to do, to smile. Sometimes it infuriated him, but most days he accepted her smile as the only shield she could offer him. If only she were British, his father would have treated her differently. And Sujoy too.

"I chose it," he said. "I chose it for its . . ."

He did not know what to say. Somehow, when exposed before his father, the Bellingshausen lost some of its appeal. Now it seemed childish, a little pond with irritating fishlets. He looked at his father and smiled, but his smile was different than his mother's—Sujoy was trying to be endearing, to win something, elicit warmth. Instead, his father stared coldly at Sujoy, and soon Sujoy did feel warm, as though he was standing in his own urine, his own beautiful piss pool.

The silence—and warmth—was broken by the ring of the doorbell. It was a shrill sound, made shriller because it was Sunday morning. As his mother answered the door, Sujoy tried to get his mind back to the ocean, but somehow the winds had changed. He closed the atlas, and was about to put it back on his father's desk when his mother came hurrying towards them.

"It's the vice-principal," she said to Sujoy's father.

"What?"

"Your colleague from work."

Sujoy glanced over at the door; it was still closed. His mother must have looked through the peephole, as was her habit.

"Are you sure?" said his father.

"Yes," his mother said. "Were you expecting him?"

Everything about his father's demeanour said no. He got up, he sat down, he got up again. He scanned his surroundings. He smoothed his white vest with his hands—although Sujoy noticed a tea stain—and he ran his fingers through his hair, flattening the strands, begging them to stick to his scalp.

"I'll get it," he said at last.

Sujoy tried to make himself look appropriate as well. Fortunately, he'd already had a bath, and was clean. He wasn't allowed to touch the atlas otherwise. He walked alongside his father towards the door, as a son should.

"What are you doing?" his father asked. "Go inside the kitchen with your mother, and don't come out."

Even though his mind questioned this command, Sujoy was surprised at how easily his body obeyed, how beautifully his father had trained him to listen. It was like his reaction when the doctor tapped his knee with a small hammer and his leg lost all control, and kicked.

A HALF-HOUR LATER, SUJOY WAS still inside the kitchen with his mother. Tea had been made, and served, and the two men were still talking. His father's voice sounded different, so welcoming—there was an expansiveness to him that Sujoy had never before witnessed.

His mother had cooked pakoras for the vice-principal, and now the pakoras were in the room with the men, but they had left their mark—oil splattered on the kitchen wall.

"Why doesn't Papa want me to go out?" he asked.

"They're talking about work," his mother said. "That's why."

"But even last month, when Uncle came over, Papa told me to go inside the kitchen. He didn't want me to come out then, either."

"He hadn't seen his brother in two years, so they had a lot to talk about."

"But Uncle wanted to see me, he kept asking for me, I could hear . . ."

Sujoy had been desperate to meet his uncle, but he dared not disobey his father's instructions. Human civilization was built on instruction, relied on instruction—or so his father had told him. What if, whilst constructing a bridge, workers did not follow the engineer's instructions? What if a nurse disobeyed a doctor? Things would go awry; serious hurt would be caused.

"Sujoy . . . would you like to learn how to cook?" His mother's voice was soft, tentative.

Cooking was the last thing on his mind. He found the kitchen a dreary place. It stank of oil and vegetables, and the small ground-floor window that looked out into the back alley only welcomed more smells. The iron grille on the window reminded Sujoy of a jail cell, so he rarely looked out of it.

"I'll teach you how to make butter chicken."

For a second, Sujoy thought he couldn't have heard correctly; perhaps he hadn't caught all of his mother's words. But no, it was a Sunday, and there was little traffic outside to disturb the forgiving silence that this one day afforded them.

"But . . . aren't we vegetarian?" he asked.

Chicken, mutton, pork, beef. Those words were rarely uttered in his father's house. His father abhorred anything that walked, moved, made sounds, had life, a heart, a soul. Even though his father spoke about dignity, about how vegetarians were respectful of life, and said that killing a living being was sinful, Sujoy knew that his father did not care a silver hoot about dogs or cats or pigeons, or anything. He wasn't cruel; but he wasn't kind.

"It'll be our secret," his mother said. There was her smile again. This time, it had a different quality to it, that of a colluder.

A secret? The flat had three tiny rooms: hall, bedroom, kitchen. What about the smell? And where would his mother find a chicken? Perhaps the heat was getting to his mother. He had often heard how, on her honeymoon, she had fainted from dehydration. His father had to carry her all the way to the local doctor. They had been in a remote village somewhere—close to his father's ancestral home—with no vehicles nearby. While Sujoy's father was carrying his mother, she had suddenly woken up in her husband's arms and said something rude to him, making fun of his face. Then she had fainted again. It had caused a huge fight between them later. This last part Sujoy had overheard his mother telling her sister one evening. Perhaps this was a similar case of babbling nonsense in the heat?

Sujoy just could not imagine his father ever carrying his mother. Maybe it was because he could not imagine his father carrying *him*. Perhaps his father might have held him when he was an infant, but at some point early on the physical contact had ceased. This was evident from his father's current relationship with him. Not once could he recall his father attending to him—to apply a Band-Aid, pat him on the head, hug him on his birthday. Verbal contact was kept to a minimum too. Except when there were instructions to be given.

"Shall we start?" his mother asked.

She removed a bowl from the fridge. Sujoy was astonished to see it was full of chicken—skinless and smooth, but soft and cold, legs and breasts covered in cream and chili powder.

"Where did you get this?" Sujoy asked. He looked out into the hall, to make sure his father was still at the table.

"Relax, that man hasn't entered the kitchen in ten years."

This would *make* him, Sujoy thought. But his mother wasn't panicking.

"First, you make a mixture of yogurt, ginger garlic paste, and red chili powder, and smear it all over the chicken," she said. "Keep it overnight. Or even an hour is fine, up to you."

"You made this last night?"

"This isn't mine. It's Leela's. Her fridge isn't working, so she kept it here last night. She has a party this evening."

"Does Papa know you have chicken in the fridge?"

"No . . . we're vegetarian, Sujoy. But I used to cook butter chicken before I got married," she said. "I used to eat it too."

Sujoy had tried chicken only once, on the sly, at a friend's birthday party two years ago. He had taken a small piece, wrapped it in a paper napkin, and gone to the bathroom to eat it, lest anyone saw. He quite liked the taste, but soon after eating it, he panicked, so he used his fingers to brush his teeth, smearing them with so much mint toothpaste that there was no chance of a lingering smell.

"Won't Leela aunty come for her chicken?" he asked.

He imagined the next-door neighbour's fat arms. She was always waving them about, the charbi underneath her biceps just as slabbery as the chicken flesh. His mother shrugged. Then she placed the boneless pieces of chicken in a pan and let them cook.

Sujoy stared at his mother. Perhaps fathers were magic killers, but who would have guessed that his mother could cast a spell?

TOMATO PURÉE, COCONUT MILK, ONIONS, red chili powder, cashew nuts, green chilies, yogurt, milk, cilantro, cumin seeds, garam masala powder, tomato ketchup . . . Sujoy's mother had pulled out all the stops. Everything was laid out before him, like in a Western movie he'd seen once, where the hero wants to buy a gun, and the owner of the joint pulls out weapon after weapon and places them on the countertop. That's what his mother was doing, she was conjuring this and that from who knew where and giving him instructions—but her instructions were so different from his father's. Hers came with a playfulness, and he had never before seen her so alive. She was enjoying herself; or perhaps it wasn't enjoyment so much as moving out of time itself, stepping out of her flat, her city, her life. Sujoy assumed this was what she was feeling because it was how he felt. Even the Bellingshausen was present; each time he opened the fridge, he felt its cold currents, its Nordic winds, and he reached out and held the glass bottles that contained chilled drinking water as if they were hope, or flowers, or springs.

In the living room, the vice-principal was still talking. When Sujoy stuck his head into the hall, he saw that a pall had fallen over his father's Sunday face, over his father's eyes and nose, and his father kept scratching an itchy palm along the edge of the table.

"What is the vice-principal saying?" Sujoy asked his mother.

"It's nothing," said his mother.

"Papa looks nervous."

"He gets like that with people from work."

Now the two men were speaking in hushed tones, and this reminded Sujoy of secrets, or of two people conspiring to hurt a third. Adults were like that. Hurtful and cowardly.

"Take that butter," his mother said. "We'll prepare the sauce now."

Sujoy took a spoonful.

"More, more," she said.

So he scooped more out of the tablespoon with his finger and let it fall into the metal pot. Then he added oil to the butter, and watched them mix, melt into each other. Next came chopped onions, ginger garlic paste, green chilies, tomatoes—all were welcome, none rebelled, not one rejected the other. Then yogurt and water. The vessel was covered, and everything was left to simmer and boil and burn.

"Slow heat," said his mother. "They need to blend into a paste."

In the other room, too, there was slow heat. When Sujoy checked, he saw that neither party was eating the snacks that had been laid out. Suddenly, he felt heavy. It was a familiar feeling, except that this time it promised to stretch on forever. He wondered how long he would live, something he hadn't ever thought about before. How many Sundays? A Sunday, then school on Monday, Tuesday, Wednesday, Thursday, Friday. Then, on Friday evening, that sad glimmer of hope before the weekend—when nothing more showed up, except the certainty of days to come.

"Ammi," he said, turning to his mother.

He saw pain dart across his mother's face, and knew what that meant—the onset of a headache. His mother got them on a regular basis and they blinded her, made her mad in the beginning and then steely, a fighter who was determined not to waste her husband's money by going to the doctor again and again only to be told to take another crocin.

As Sujoy watched carefully, she strained the mixture in the pot to see if any pulpy bits remained. Satisfied, she put the sauce back and let it boil on a high flame. The gas stove suddenly showed its temper, the volcanic flames rising with that beautiful *whoop* sound, and when Sujoy closed his eyes, he imagined wings, opening and closing, making those same sounds. He breathed deep, accepting the smell of the kitchen. All the ingredients were now speaking to him, throwing bits of themselves at him, the way flowers were sprinkled on a just-married couple, only here there was no love . . . No, he thought, there *is* love, there is son and mother, and for the first time the son is discovering the mother, and she is revealing herself to him, the ingredients that make her.

Sujoy opened his eyes. Next came cashew paste, then sugar. Always sugar. In tea, in food, in cake, those bits of white, doppelgängers of salt, double agents—they were always needed. And then: ketchup. Sujoy's mother handed him the bottle and he slammed it against his palm, and the ketchup oozed out—one, two—and he hit the bottle a third time, liking the forcefulness.

"Sujoy," she said. "My head is—"

"I know," he said. "I know."

He said this tenderly, and his mother smiled at him. This was a third smile: neither weak nor colluding, it was the smile of gratitude. Gratitude for his understanding. Suddenly, his heart opened, and he was so confused that he grabbed his mother and gave her a tight hug. She let him stay there, leaning against her, and patted the back of his head, then rubbed his hair down, setting it straight, although for what occasion he didn't know.

"Don't worry," she said. "Everything will be all right."

Instead of calm, anxiety sprang forth within him like music, drums and rumbles that disturbed the rhythm of his daily life. His mother had never before addressed his anxiety, and now that she had tried to assuage it, he felt even more jittery than usual. His mind spewed a hundred questions, but none of them were audible; instead they created roads inside him, roads leading nowhere.

"It's okay not to love someone," she said.

These words hit him—slapped him, rejuvenated him. They seemed to come out of nowhere, but he instinctively understood their meaning. Yes, perhaps the father didn't love the son; that much he had guessed. But she wasn't talking about Sujoy. She was talking about herself. His mother didn't love the man she had married. And Sujoy realized he was overjoyed to hear this. But there was no feeling of celebration within him; it was a sullen joy. Joy could be sullen.

His mother turned away, and took the chicken out of the fridge. Her movements were slow, and Sujoy could see that the headache was catching up to her, eating its way into the back of her neck. Her eyes were drowsy, her eyelids swollen.

"Will you handle the rest?" she asked.

Sujoy knew she was talking about the chicken—but she was also telling him to take charge. Of his life, his movements. Particularly his movements.

He looked at the way she herself moved, suddenly so tired, dishevelled, almost swaying, but not the way a tree sways in the wind. There was a lack of grace in her movements, and a stinking resignation. A hot stink, the kind that one received in Bombay every so often when an open garbage truck passed by, debris coming off it—dirty plastic bags like confetti. His mother was discarding something in a similar fashion, all the hours, minutes, days spent with this man— they were flying off her shoulders and into Sujoy's face. They were an omen, and the message was clear: if he didn't do something, he would stink too.

He watched his mother enter the bedroom and lie down. The sudden tigress, the spell-caster, had become ordinary again, apologetic, so light she hardly made a dent in the mattress. She took a pillow, groaned, and covered her eyes with it. And when she covered her eyes, Sujoy felt darkness envelop him. He should run away—but where could he go? He didn't have a single friend. Just a week ago, two boys at school, tough types, the bullies that everyone aspired to be, had come up to him during recess and asked, "Sujoy, do you want to be our friend?" Sujoy's eyes had lit up, and his heart had swelled with such big hope and relief that he immediately cried *yes* with all his might, only to hear them say, "But what makes you think we want to be yours?" The laughter rang in his ears so loud that when the last school bell sounded three hours later he bolted to his bus like an athlete, something he had never been. On the bus, he had realized that he was going home to a father he could never talk to about this experience. But today, on this Sunday afternoon, his mother had reached out her hand to him, and he was determined not to let her down.

He stared at the bowl, at the dead bird that would be his and his mother's deliverance. He massaged the chicken, mixed the cold cream into its skin some more, and watched as the red chili powder made his fingers bleed. With each touch he loved the taste, the taste of the touch; there was a direct connection between his brain and fingers, bypassing the tongue entirely. He pushed his fingers into the breast of the chicken and the breast bounced back, as if it was daring him to cook it, to finish it, to get the job done. Sweat was rolling down his cheek and forehead and he wished he had his mother's sari to wipe it away. He loved that particular movement, the total naturalness of it, compared with the clumsy movements of his father—the way his father was nervously shaking his legs right now, in fact, when Sujoy peeked at him in the next room.

Everything, he understood, was about movement. What movement did he need to execute now?

He overturned the contents of the bowl into the container and let the flesh cook and scream its way back to life. There, one movement accomplished. "Done," he said to himself, and his voice purred out of him. He loved hearing it; it was not a sound he had ever made before. He looked at the chicken again, the bubbles in its skin large and round, bursting into air. Then he heard his father's voice, calling out to his mother. The vice-principal was leaving. Would she come out and say goodbye?

Did his father smell the chicken? Sujoy wondered. Surely he must smell the chicken.

He saw his mother slowly raise her arm. She could hardly speak, and she didn't even bother to pull the pillow away from her eyes. Sujoy gave his fingers a quick rinse, went into the bedroom, held his mother's hand, and gently tried to tug her out of bed. Once again his father's voice, irritated now, was calling for her.

"You go . . ." she said to Sujoy. Her voice was weak and soft, a feather falling on a carpet.

Sujoy wasn't allowed to go out into the main room. She knew that. And yet she wanted him to respond to his father's call, to complete the movement. He tried to gather his courage to step out, but he felt ashamed, backed into a corner. He could feel his resolve and strength waning. If he didn't rise today, he never would, but he needed something to help—his mother's hand, his mother's strength. Sujoy's own hand was still grasping his mother's wrist, her green bangles. When his father called out her name a third time, Sujoy pulled off his mother's bangles, pushed them over his wrists, and walked out of the kitchen into the hall. He felt like someone on display in a world of courtiers and jesters, and at last he walked just as he wanted to, as he felt inside, not caring a silver hoot about what his father thought. And his father's face, that Sunday face, changed shape, lost its form, and crumpled.

"THE THING IS, THE VICE-PRINCIPAL had come over to tell my father that his services were no longer required," Sujoy said to the audience. He could only see the faces in the first row, but the woman right in front of him seemed to understand what he was saying. He wondered where she was from; he guessed Kansas. The room was cold, and Gupta's Butter Chicken was almost done.

"My mother died a few months later," he said. "The headaches were because of a tumour, but in those days . . ." He trailed off. He was giving them a real show, a chef with heart. James must be loving it; he could feel James's approval. The host carefully tried to jut in, but Sujoy carried on, he needed to complete the inevitable tidal movement. "But she didn't want to waste his money," he said. "So she's dead, and that prick is still alive."

"Well . . ." said the host. "We'll have to . . ."

"I have to complete the movement," he replied.

"I'm sorry?"

"The movement," he said.

He went ahead then, and did what he'd done back then, after the vice-principal had left, after his father had slapped him hard across the face, the back, then the face again, and the legs too, his father covering every inch of his body, as if his body were a map and his father the most adventurous, daring explorer. His mother had come out of the room, even with her headache, and taken one or two blows herself.

Now Sujoy dipped his palms into the paste he had made and showed them to the audience. Palms of purée, palms of milk, palms of chili powder, palms of cilantro, palms of ketchup. Palms from more than thirty years ago. Back then, he had marinated those hands, "fetched" his father's atlas, opened it to a random page, and smeared it, an act that had given him a sense of delight unmatched by any lover since.

As the woman from Kansas looked away, Sujoy stared above the heads of the silent audience, past the bright lights, towards his father, that unreachable god who lurked in the dark uncharted waters beyond.

MR. MOLT

Reshma looked at her wrist, then realized she had stopped wearing a watch a long time ago. She had her iPhone in her lap, but she didn't really want to know the time. She was just impatient because her driver had stopped the car to use the public urinal, and he hadn't returned. It wasn't the waiting; it was the stench. Even though the windows were rolled up and the AC was on, nothing could keep the foulness away.

She regretted leaving the house. She hadn't left the house in three months. She knew she wasn't ready, but Bakul had insisted. And when Bakul Gawande insisted, human beings wilted. That was what had attracted her to him in the first place, that he didn't have to exert his might, or resort to the cartoonish histrionics some of his contemporaries displayed. He was a born overlord; there was something within him, some gene, that made people listen. Men, especially. Women could occasionally drive him batty and make him maudlin. It was he who had insisted she go to the salon today and get her hair done—sitting in the dark wasn't doing her any good. He had promised to accompany her and stay at the salon the entire time, but had backed out at the last minute because he had to engineer a hit. An opportunity had come up and he needed to oversee the operation. That was his key word: "I have to *oversee*," he would always say. "If I don't *oversee*, things go wrong."

Well, they had. For both of them. And no amount of *overseeing* had made any difference. Just like the red roses that were painted on the walls of the urinal made no difference to the stench. Her husband and she were both red roses.

Reshma's phone rang. The tune of its ringer filled up the inside of the car like temple bells. She immediately switched it off; she wanted nothing to do with temple bells. They reminded her of how she had begged and prayed, how she had prostrated herself before every god, a sapling begging for water, until her stem broke, and she had collapsed onto the ground.

Even though the phone had stopped ringing, the sound remained in her memory, suffocating her. She reached into her handbag for her anti-anxiety medication. She liked the name: Zapiz. It had a magical feel to it, 0.25 mg of some fairy dust that prevented her from tearing her hair out. It was clear now that her driver had gone for a shit. Not a piss, as he had mentioned; he had lied to her out of embarrassment, perhaps. What did it matter? Piss or shit, he was lucky—it would be out of his system in no time. In her case, loss had found a permanent home inside her. It had immigrated there, crossing the borders and walls of her heart, threatening to remain forever. She hated the feeling of heart-pounding terror that currently occupied her breast, until the Zapiz kicked in. She needed some air. She pressed a button and the window of her black Audi rolled down smoothly, providing the perfect opening for the shameless pungency of the urinal.

Just as she realized her mistake, and was about to roll the window back up, something caught her eye. Pasted on the wall of the urinal, far above the roses, was a cartoon sketch of a penguin. He had a big smile on his face. It unnerved her. Not the smile itself, but there was something about the penguin, some familiarity she could not identify. It was as though he was looking directly at her. She rolled the window up, and then down again, immediately. She kept pressing the button, and up and down the window went, showing her that face, then taking it away, showing it to her, taking it away, and each time it was taken away, she felt a longing for it, and, equally, an immense stupidity. She knew she shouldn't have gone out of the house.

The door on the driver's side suddenly opened, and there was Lalit. He seemed relieved, as people do when they have been to the toilet after an unbearable urge; they are like people who have won the lottery. Lalit's expression signified that he had won more than enough to buy a plush apartment in any part of Bombay. Truly a shitload of cash, she thought. It made her smile. The smile brought her no joy, but at least the shape of her mouth and lips had changed for the first time in three months.

"Sorry, madam," he said sheepishly.

She did not reply. She was just waiting for the Zapiz to work. She would take a Restyl when she got home. One calmed you down, the other made you sleepy. Together, they made you forget.

She kept the window down as the car moved, not caring that the breeze undid her hairdresser's hour-and-a-half of work at the salon. In fact she welcomed it, inviting it to tangle her hair up, dishevel it as much as possible, so that she could go home to Bakul that way. She passed by the Byculla vegetable market, and a restaurant that her husband's rival, Ahmed, owned. It was funny: both Bakul and Ahmed called themselves restaurateurs even though they didn't know the first thing about food. But they owned so many restaurants in the city—it was one of the best ways to launder money—they had started believing they were arbiters of good taste. Bakul dealt in vegetarian cuisine while Ahmed had a chain of non-veg lounges called Panther Heart. He used a strong animal name to position himself as the true king of Mumbai, unlike his Hindu rival, who took a more spiritual approach to restaurant names: Tantra, Lotus, Blue Sky. Reshma wondered what Ahmed's wives were like. He had three. But only one showed herself in public, or was perhaps allowed to. Were any of his wives on Zapiz?

The car slowed down, waiting for the handcarts and cycles to get out of the way so that they could turn left on S-Bridge.

Once again, he was there.

A small penguin, smiling at her from his place high atop a lightpole. Reshma squinted to read the print that ran below his feet: *Humboldt Penguins at Byculla Zoo.* There he was, looking at her, beguiling her. He was utterly stupid, and yet . . . there was an innocence to him that drew her in. He had a bit of a tummy, just a bit—perhaps that's where he stashed his joy, where his secret reserves of happiness lay, enabling him to keep smiling like that. She could picture him rubbing his tummy and laughing, sending out a sound way more soothing and truthful than temple bells.

She looked at her wrist again. Once again, she did not need to know the time; it was pure habit. She had nowhere to go, nowhere to be. Only her bedroom beckoned, its darkness and shadows her companions—but they would always be there. She was struck by this thing in front of her, this soft, happy thing in black and white that gave off so much colour. If a picture could do this, a mere sketch, what might the actual being do?

"Lalit," she said. "Go straight."

"Madam?"

"Don't take a left, go straight and make a U-turn from the signal."

"Did you forget something at the salon?"

That was the problem with Lalit. With all drivers. They all needed to know more than they needed to know.

"Just do as I say," she said.

He accelerated the car as a form of protest, his ego bruised by being barked at, that too by a woman. After all, Lalit had once been Bakul's driver-cum-bodyguard, feared by all who knew him. But he was now a reformed man, of his own accord. He had told Bakul that he would no longer stab anyone or even hit them, except in self-defence; but he would gladly take a bullet for Bakul. Of this, there was no doubt. Bakul inspired that kind of loyalty. He looked after his people, and their families. If only he had been able to look after his own.

Even though the car was stopped at the red light, Lalit kept pressing and releasing the accelerator. The Audi felt like the sizzling black body of a creature in the afternoon heat. A creature ready to slide away from the rest of humanity. Once again, Reshma's heart thudded: she had spotted three large penguins underneath the Byculla bridge, right opposite the Zoroastrian fire temple. Huge plastic bodies with curving beaks. How had she not noticed them before? Perhaps they had just sprung up during the past three months of her self-imposed exile. She wondered when penguins had first wandered the Earth. Had anyone noticed them? *Was* there anyone to notice? Unlike the baby penguin on the poster for the zoo, these plastic penguins did not soothe her; there was something sinister about them. Was it the fact that they were adults? No, no, it was the way they looked, their posture, the defiant manner in which they leaned their heads towards the sky, as if incanting something in a language unknown to her, the same way the Zoroastrian priests chanted their prayers in a tongue that was foreign to her ears, and to the ears of anyone belonging to another religion.

Lalit took a very sharp U-turn. Reshma decided to give in. She would give him the coordinates he so desperately sought.

"I want to go to the zoo," she said.

"The zoo?"

There it was again. The redundant, idiotic retort of a man who knew how to use a knife but not his brain.

"Yes, the zoo," she said. "The *Byculla* zoo."

More coordinates. More specificity. More fodder for the male ego. Lalit seemed pleased with the information. Before he could ask why she wanted to go to the zoo, she told him.

"I need to take some pictures of the garden. They have done it up very well. I saw a photograph in the paper a few days ago."

"Oh," said Lalit. "I think I did too."

No, you did not, she wanted to say. Because there was no photograph.

"Wasn't it lovely?" she asked.

"Yes, madam."

"I want to do something like that for my Khandala property."

"Okay, madam," he said.

When the Audi approached the zoo gate, the security guard immediately saluted the car. He shooed away a bunch of school kids who were in the way.

"Park here," she said to Lalit. "And go have some lunch."

"I should go with you."

"No, I need to be alone."

"But Dada will—"

"He will nothing," said Reshma. "And don't bother calling him, because he's in the middle of something."

Lalit nodded. Reshma figured he knew about the hit. He was still part of the "setting" committee, the ones who orchestrated the hit. Logistics, timings, shooting or stabbing, disposal of the body, et cetera—all of it had to be engineered with precision, and the members of the committee had to devise a plan, a blueprint they then handed over to the men on the assembly line. Lalit was reformed; therefore, he did not execute. But he still orchestrated.

Before the car came to a complete standstill, Reshma grabbed her purse, opened the door, and walked to the ticket counter. She had not felt this energized since forever. And it wasn't really energy; it was a gasp of air, a sudden inhalation that confirmed that perhaps she was still alive. Fifty rupees was all she had to pay. To feel again, something, anything, she would have paid a crore.

"Does this entry include the penguins?" she asked.

"Just follow the signs," said the man at the counter, without looking at her. He was busy arranging the currency into neat stacks.

It occurred to Reshma that she had been doing this anyway. Following the signs. The penguin on the urinal, then the same face next to Panther Heart, then the adult plastic penguins underneath the bridge, their mouths open, shaman-like. What did it all mean? Where were they leading her?

She could feel a quiver in her thighs, which could be interpreted as a sign too, a sign that she was heading in the wrong direction, that no good could come from all this. But what else did she have? She was a pathetic moron. Only morons followed impulses, she reckoned. The wires in her brain had received a terrible shock, and they were trying to reconfigure themselves. She should give them time before she ventured out into the world again. As she passed through the metal detectors to enter the main zoo, she could feel a current hum within her, signalling an impasse of sorts. She was being given a chance to turn back. She waited, not caring that she held up the line.

"Please move ahead," said the guard on duty.

Reshma just stood there, feeling the hum. Then she decided to keep going.

It had been years since she had been to the zoo. Decades. The last time she'd been here was with her father. He would bring her to listen to the birds and to see the crocodiles. Birds and crocodiles. Both God's creations, he used to say. But so, so different. One airborne, celebratory. The other a crawling adver-tisement for all that is decayed—an angry, ruthless being, whose only aim is to end things. A crocodile is a full stop, a bird is a continuation. Now she understood what her father had meant.

She soon found herself right in front of the statues of a young Shivaji and his mother, Veermata Jijamata Bhosale, whom the zoo was named after. What had once been Rani Baug —the Queen's Gardens—was now named, rightly so, after the Maratha warrior's mother. Even in stone, she looked so graceful. Shivaji, as a boy, was in the process of drawing his sword, while she gently placed her hands on his shoulders, protecting him, nurturing him.

Why did Reshma's hands have no power? Why had her prayers, so real and desperate, had no effect on her son's health?

All Jijamata had done was place her hands on her son and it had inspired him to form the Maratha Empire, become a warrior unlike any India had ever seen. All of this because of his mother's blessing. Reshma too had tried to bless her son; day and night she had placed her hand on his forehead, cursing the fever, then begging it, then threatening it, then pleading again, but nothing had worked.

She felt sick. This zoo visit was a terrible idea. All it had done was pinpoint her shortcomings as a mother. The rage started rising within her. She needed to hurt herself. She reached into her handbag and took out her nail cutter and began to make cuts on her forearm, like someone who desperately wanted to satisfy an itch, except that the itch was total evisceration. She felt some relief as the blood trickled, tiny streams of justice. She kept at it until she felt the pain deeply, until it made her eyes well up.

"Mummy," she heard someone say.

A young girl was staring at her. She was pointing Reshma out to her mother, who was looking at Reshma, aghast.

"Can you tell me where the penguins are?" Reshma asked the woman. She put the nail cutter back into her handbag, casually, so as not to alarm the girl any further. This was not something the little girl should have seen. But why was the child staring at humans? Why wasn't she looking at the animals?

The woman pointed into the distance. "Thank you," was all Reshma said.

Once she was a fair distance away, she stopped and called Lalit. Screw the penguins. Screw those black-and-white miserable plumpy fuckheads. But Lalit wasn't answering his phone. She called him again, and again. He was out to lunch and so was his damn phone. She had told Bakul not to assign Lalit to her, but did Bakul listen? To anything? There was no use going back to the car. She would probably take a small rock and smash the window of the Audi if Lalit wasn't around. It was best to march on.

It wasn't hard to find the penguin enclosure. The path towards it was lined with plastic facsimiles, like little watchmen grinning away, still as a moment, still as life in shock. These plastic birds led her to a blue building.

HUMBOLDT PENGUINS

The sign was huge. The penguins were the star attraction of the zoo, no doubt. There was a substantial crowd in front of the enclosure, and the lineup was long and winding, like the rest of Reshma's life. She stood, waiting her turn. She wiped the blood on her wrist with her handkerchief, and then dabbed her lips with the cloth as well.

Lalit was phoning her back. She didn't answer. Let him worry.

When at last she entered the building, she felt a change in temperature. It was much colder inside, like her room at home, which was always colder than the rest of the house. Around her were scores of children, and mothers, and fathers, all expectant, all so eager.

Her excitement had died, and had been replaced with a low, grumbling feeling of confusion. She felt disoriented amidst the pitter-patter of small feet. The sound would have been sweet if it were not for the fact that none of those feet had any connection to her. Her head drooped, and she nudged the man in front of her with her handbag. He was walking too slowly. The attendant checked her ticket again, and asked the woman behind her to put her cellphone away.

"No photo allowed," he said.

She could now see the glass enclosure, one-fourth of it filled with clear water.

The air was thick with oohs and aahs and mummies pointing this way and that, and daddies holding toddlers, kissing them, extra . . . extra kisses in this air-conditioned room. When the penguins came into Reshma's line of sight, she felt momentarily dizzy. They were swimming from one end to the next in a flurry. Some of them were sliding along the glass, their bellies rubbing against it, releasing small bubbles as they travelled.

How many were there? She counted four.

The cop on duty kept blowing a whistle, to keep the line moving, and this irritated her. She spotted two more penguins standing on the rock surface, facing the audience. They reminded her of the adult, plastic ones she had seen earlier near the fire temple, and suddenly everything made sense. The penguin parents were sending out a chant from underneath the bridge, a call to action, and their kids were responding in a frenzy, swimming up and down like battery dolls. If the enclosure had been more silent, she would have been able to hear their incantation, but the crowd was so noisy, so enthralled by this circus, they missed hearing the chant completely. Now the two penguins that had been standing jumped into the water and joined the other four. The six of them were swimming from one end to the other. The cop blew his whistle, asking people to move along in a single file; there were others waiting to get in. For once, Reshma was grateful for a cop. She wanted to get the hell out.

She was a few feet away from the exit when she saw something red flash before her eyes. The source of the flash was hiding behind a boulder. He was wearing a red T-shirt. He was taking a peek at the crowd, like a child playing hide-and-seek. So human he was. She froze when she saw his face. That familiarity again . . . it was the penguin on the poster, no doubt about it. Suddenly, she felt a serenity, a quiet thank you, but . . . for what? Was it from him to her, or from her to him?

A shrill whistle disturbed her reverie. The cop was looking at her and blowing it, and a female cop came forward and held Reshma's hand.

"Madam, please move," she said.

"But . . . I'm not done."

"Please move," the female cop said again, firmly this time. "You can rejoin the line and come back from outside."

Reshma was furious. Not because she cared about being asked to move but because the penguin had disappeared. She wanted to slap the cop. Could the cop not see what had been transpiring? That a moment had been born, between her and that little boy?

She stomped her way round the building and got in line again. But this time she did not wait. She strode ahead of everyone else with an intent so fierce that no one dared question her. When the attendant opened his mouth to protest, she told him, "Someone stole my wallet."

He looked at the handbag she was holding.

"This is a handbag," she said. "My purse is missing."

Not wanting to argue, sensing that this woman was moneyed and therefore important, the attendant let her pass.

"Who is the one in the red T-shirt?" Reshma asked him.

"Oh, that's Mr. Molt," said the attendant.

"Who?"

"Mr. Molt. That's his name. It's his birthday today, so he was made to wear a T-shirt."

The six penguins were all in the water, and the little one could not be seen. The others were now in a complete tizzy; Reshma was sure that the shamans from underneath the bridge were controlling these penguins. But to what end? Couldn't they see that they were driving their own children up the wall, literally? The penguins were almost banging into the glass, as if they were trying to slide *up*, against the glass, into the crowd, into freedom. But the crowd was not freedom, she wanted to tell them. Anything but. Crowds were cold and insensitive. Or overbearing. But this was not her business. She was only interested in Mr. Molt. No, she would not call him that. It was too cold a name.

She stood in the middle of the line and refused to budge. She got a few dirty stares, but her stare was dirtier. Soon, all stares dissolved. When the cop blew his whistle again, she blew back. She pointed to a sign that had been posted by the authorities on the glass: *No loud noises. They disturb the Humboldt penguins.*

"You're scaring them!" she said. "Can't you follow your own rule?"

The crowd moved away from her like ripples from a stone that has just been tossed into the water. Reshma looked for the little one again.

"Please," she whispered. "Don't be scared . . ."

But he didn't come. He could not hear her.

"It's me," she said.

She could hear herself. She knew how she sounded, knew exactly what she was saying. She felt herself sinking into the ground—because maybe that was the only thing left to do, to sink into the ground and emerge in the penguin enclosure, and rise to the surface through the water to reach him.

She felt the world spin, and held tight to the railing.

Once again, red revealed itself, a bright flash against a different pillar. The little one was scared.

"Come out," she said. "Show yourself to me."

There was only him and her now. Slowly, inch by inch, he came forward.

"There's the birthday boy!" said someone from the crowd.

The man next to her was singing, "Happy birthday, happy birthday." The little one now showed himself fully, and she felt something enlarge within her, as if she was being stretched, given new cells. He stood stationary, right opposite her.

Once again that beautiful familiarity, as if she was listening to a song she had heard a long time ago but forgotten.

He was unlike his brothers and sisters—and Reshma suddenly felt certain he wasn't their sibling, just as the penguins under the bridge weren't his mother and father. That's why he was not responding to their call. He was responding to Reshma's.

Still, she had to be sure.

She looked at him now, with a promise so solid, a promise that said, *If it is you,* *then this time I won't let anything happen to you. You have my word.*

What would his response be? How could he possibly show her that it might be him? That it *was* him?

And then, he did the unthinkable.

He turned around and revealed his bum to the audience.

"It *is* you," Reshma gasped. "Oh my God, it is you."

He used to do the same thing when he faced a crowd. When scores of relatives came over to see him, to wish him a happy birthday—but not out of affection; out of fear and respect, and the need to be in Bakul Gawande's good books—he had, out of sheer contrariness, showed his butt to them all. The situation had been exactly the same:

A crowd was singing "Happy Birthday."

A crowd was staring at him.

No photographs were allowed then, either, because Bakul did not allow photographs to be taken inside his home.

And he had worn a red T-shirt.

Reshma would go to him, whisk him up in her arms, and carry him back to his room. How he had smiled. How he had gurgled and laughed, like a fountain.

There was no doubt now. This was her Keshu.

And Keshu wanted her to rescue him.

She blew him a kiss through the glass. "I will be with you soon," she said. "Don't you worry, Mummy has found you."

BAKUL GAWANDE HAD NEVER BEEN this worried. Not even when he had stabbed a man for the first time. It was the expression on the man's face that had scared him, the man's realization that these were the last few seconds of his life. Moreover, the man had been an acquaintance, so Gawande had wanted to say something to him while the knife was inside him, something to the effect of, "It's not personal," or "This will be over soon." Something like that. But before he could say anything, the knife had done its job. Then he'd had to run.

But when it came to Reshma, he couldn't run. He had plenty of time to say things to her, to reason with her, but nothing made a difference. It was the expression on her face that terrified him. Unlike the man he had killed, Reshma grew stronger by the minute. Stronger and calmer. So resolute in her intention, a general at war. Now was the time to strike, she seemed to say. Keshu needs us. Before now, she had stopped uttering his name. Even when she had sobbed at night, there were just cries, yells, directed at the skies and the pillows. If he'd tried to soothe her, she screamed more. But now she mentioned her son's name with disturbing calm.

Bakul was seated in the living room, his purohit opposite him. He sipped his single malt, but all it did was hurt his throat. The purohit was in his white dhoti and bare-chested, with his sacred thread around him, but he too looked perplexed.

"Tell me what to do," asked Bakul.

"I . . . I don't know," said the purohit.

You don't know? Bakul wanted to throw the single malt across the man's tiny face. The purohit was the one who had started all this. "Your son will come back to you," he had said to Reshma. "Love like that always finds its way back."

And now he didn't know what to do?

"My suggestion is that you play along," said the purohit.

"She came back with cuts on her wrist!" Bakul lowered his voice. Reshma was in the bedroom, and the door was closed, but he did not want her to hear him.

"It has given her hope. It would be dangerous to take it away."

"Why can't you people think before you speak? Why would you tell her that our son will come back?"

"Sir, we believe in reincarnation . . ."

"So do I. But every time I have someone killed, I don't tell him, 'Listen, it's okay, you'll come back.' Do I?"

The purohit decided it was best to stay silent.

"Is there anything in your scriptures that speaks of how animals will remain animals and not ever become human?"

"Sir, at this point, no matter what I say, your wife will believe only what she wants to believe. She was not very religious anyway, if you remember. It's just that she's now choosing to . . ." The purohit trailed off. He did not want to judge the woman. She was in the throes of grief, so animalistic it mauled you and left you reeling forever. He had seen people cope in different ways. Some clung to God, some to holy books, others to drink, some took their own lives, others sang devotional songs and claimed they saw colours, and some became humbled by the experience and entered into service for their fellow human beings. This, however, was new.

"It's unknown how she will react if you don't follow through," he said. "It is my suggestion that you do whatever you can."

"I'd like you to speak with her."

"Sir, what can I—"

"You started this. You end it. Tell her it's all bakwaas."

"Sir, I . . . I can't. This is a kind of devotion. An unusual love from an unusual person."

"What the hell are you talking about?"

"It might seem like rubbish. But there is a purity in it . . . she is reaching a state that very few souls experience."

Bakul reflected that he badly wanted the priest to experience an altered state too. One created by smashing his head with a cricket bat. But he told himself to calm down.

How quickly the day had turned. It was meant to be a day of exultation.

By successfully eliminating Ahmed, owner of Panther Heart, Bakul was now the undisputed don of the city, and yet here he was, sitting in his living room, cowering before his wife's whims and fancies. He missed his son too. But this—this was beyond the human heart. This was debauchery.

He got up from the sofa with a jerk that made the purohit nervous.

"Come," he said. "You will come with me. We will go to the bedroom and we will reason with her."

He placed his hand on the purohit's shoulder and was surprised by how cold it was. Why the guy didn't wear a shirt, even in an air-conditioned room, was something Bakul could never understand. Maybe he should have offered the purohit a shawl. Hell, he would give him ten shawls, all pashminas, if he could put some sense into his wife. He would import ten sheep from New Zealand and the purohit could make the wool himself if he so wished.

Bakul knocked on the door and waited for a response. No answer.

He slowly opened the door, and led them both into the dimness of the room. But it wasn't as dark as usual. His wife wasn't lying in bed, either. She was sitting in a chair, her back upright, with a table lamp next to her, and she was doing something with her hands. He followed his wife's gaze to the wall above their bed. Shadows were in play there, forming, thanks to the movements of his wife's hands, what looked like a duck. There was a distinct beak, no doubt. Then she got the shape right, and it made his skin crawl. A baby penguin was walking on the wall.

THE PUPPETRY CONTINUED FOR an hour more, and Bakul had no choice but to send the purohit home. Sick of seeing nonsensical shapes on the wall, he quietly slunk into bed and waited patiently for his wife to end the show. She eventually did, and even wished him good night, and he responded with a strained good night of his own.

Now, as Bakul lay sleepless, he thought of how the grief had not punished him the way it had his wife. Then again, she had wanted a child with more ferocity than him. She had fucked him with the hunger of someone who needed air and water. And she had waited for Keshu for years, and had consulted the same purohit, who had said to her, "He will come." And the boy did. The purohit got the gender right too. But now, for Reshma to latch on to something he'd said to console her . . . this was unholy.

Suddenly, Reshma sprang up like a spring.

"I want to show you something," she said. She reached for her iPad, and its screen lit up the room with a phosphorescence that made Bakul think of caves. What this light would discover, or illuminate, was going to be eerie.

She clicked on a link that led to the *Times of India*:
PENGUIN AT MUMBAI'S BYCULLA ZOO DIES.

"Reshma . . ." Bakul reached his hand out, very slowly, to touch his wife. But she blocked his hand with hers.

"Bakul, please. If you love me, just see what it says."

Bakul put the iPad in his lap. He felt as though he was holding something poisonous, something so pernicious that its bearer was doomed the minute he stared into its light. There had been eight Humboldt penguins at one point. Imports from Seoul. Last year, one of them had died. Before they even went on display, the penguins had lost a sister.

"That's sad," he said, "but I—"

"Greenish stools, Bakul."

"What?"

"She had greenish stools."

"So?"

"Before Keshu got sick, before the fever went berserk, his stools were green."

Bakul sighed.

Reshma did not expect him to understand. She had hoped he would, but she did not expect him to. A mother's love is always deeper than a father's. A mother will go to any length to save her child, to bring him back. Men were weak; they did not go the distance. If they could, nature would have endowed them with the ability to bear life, to carry it within the womb like a small planet. What did Bakul know of love, of how Keshu had orbited in her belly for months? What did he know of the feeling it gave her, a sense of purpose so clear, devotion had a whole new meaning?

"Bakul," she said. "A mosquito got the better of you."

"Reshma, please."

"I'm not blaming you," she said. "All I'm saying is that the dengue was due to a mosquito. Doesn't that tell you something?"

How well his wife knew him, Bakul thought. Even though he had given his son the best treatment, dengue was unpredictable. It took away and spared, spared and took away, depending on its mood. Reshma sensed exactly what he thought and how he felt, even though he never voiced it. She knew that he, the indomitable Bakul Gawande, ruthless disposer of destinies, was dealt the severest blow by a mere mosquito.

Bakul looked into the light again. He was not reading the article but trying to find something in the beams emanating from the iPad, some respite, some grain of truth or common sense that he could impart to his wife. He got nothing, so he just slid his finger along the screen and kept reading. There was a comment from one Jignesh Shah: "What was the need to rob these beautiful creatures of their natural habitat in the first place? To entertain our Mumbaikars?!?!" How right this man is, thought Bakul. Why couldn't the zoo stick with lions and elephants? Where had this sudden urge for penguins come from?

"Reshma . . . I miss him too, you know," he said.

"I know . . ."

But Reshma longed to tell him so much more. How, after reading about one penguin's death, she was now certain that the other penguins beneath the bridge were sending a signal to their children because they did not want them to die as well. How penguins in the water were called a *raft*, while on land they were a *waddle*. Keshu had never entered the water; he hated having a bath, and he cried when water touched his skin. This proved that the raft of six penguins had nothing to do with the seventh! The seventh was waiting to waddle his way back into Reshma's life. Would Bakul understand? Was he open enough?

"After Keshu, I felt I could not even breathe. I felt there was a rope around my neck and it was choking me. Now he wants to come back to us. Don't let there be one more death," she said. "Please, Bakul. I beg you."

IT WAS UP TO LALIT to get the guns inside the zoo.

The recent arrival of the penguins had meant beefed-up security, and this was going to make it extremely challenging, but the solution to Lalit's problem lay in the beautification plans for the zoo gardens. Just before one passed through the metal detectors, there was a display of animals—all of them plastic —owl, tiger, parrot, eagle, and monkey, perched on a wall and arranged in a semicircle facing the public. Below them, there were replicas of the Humboldt penguins. A man was painting them, adding big splashes of white to their bellies. Lalit saw him enter the zoo with his bag of brushes and paint—and without passing through the metal detectors. With cash and threats, Lalit convinced this man to place the guns at the feet of a giant mouse in the zoo. The mouse was covered in fake grass and zebra flowers, and he instructed the man to dig a hole directly underneath the mouse's ass and cover it up with more fake flowers. Easy for the hit men to find.

But first, the hit men, Mohan and Tapas, needed to survey the penguin enclosure. The two of them were relatively new to the Gawande gang, but they had accomplished a lot in five short years and had it not been for the fact that Gawande himself had briefed them on their task, they would have felt deeply insulted at the ridiculousness of the undertaking. When they saw their boss hem and haw, almost at a loss for words, as he described the assignment, they had realized how important it must be.

Tapas, the younger of the two, was always being scolded by Mohan—something Tapas resented. Just because he was younger did not mean he could be chided day in and day out. Tapas did not have a formal education, but he was convinced that his ideas were superior. Mohan and he were the founding members of the Fatka gang. As twenty-somethings, they had run alongside railway tracks with the speed of cheetahs and administered "fatkas" with sticks—sharp, electric hits on a commuter's hand, the one holding the mobile phone—thereby making the commuter drop the phone onto the tracks, which the gang members then picked up and sold on the black market. Their start-up was thriving until one day Mohan and Tapas made the mistake of giving a fatka to one of Gawande's men. He hunted them down over the next few days, and administered some grand whacks in return, but eventually "all's well that ends well"—or at least, that's what Gawande told the boys when he recruited them. He liked their enterprising nature, he said, and their ability to take a severe beating.

"Look," said Mohan. "There's the mouse."

"Is that Mickey Mouse?"

"No," said Mohan. "It's just some unknown mouse."

Tapas looked at the mouse again, but the fake grass and flowers that ran up and over its face made it difficult to discern its features.

"I think it's Mickey," he said.

"Who cares?"

A young couple was taking a picture of themselves with the mouse using a selfie stick. This spot had been designated as a "Selfie Point" by the zoo authorities.

"Why would you want a photo with a mouse?" asked Tapas.

"Why would you want a penguin in your house?" asked Mohan.

Tapas had no answer to that. Neither he nor Mohan had dared question Gawande about the strangeness of his order. "Get Mr. Molt," was all he had said. Tapas wondered if it had anything to do with the fact that Valentine's Day was just around the corner. Maybe Gawande wanted to do something unique for his wife. Maybe Mrs. Gawande—Didi, as the men called her—was tired of receiving Gucci handbags and perfume. There was no doubt that Mr. Molt would be unlike anything she had ever received.

Mr. Molt.

When Tapas thought about a penguin with that name, the image of a short, strict man wearing a tuxedo and bow tie came to mind. There would be something regal about the chap, like a butler in an English film. What did butlers do if, whilst serving dinner, their underwear got stuck in the cracks of their arses?

"So many cops around," remarked Mohan.

But Tapas wasn't looking at the cops. He was staring at a couple who were smooching. The man had his hands around the woman's waist, which was lusciously exposed by the gap in her violet sari.

"Are you listening?" asked Mohan. "Focus."

"When we reach America, I will get a woman from all nationalities. I mean, a woman each from each nationality—"

"I get it."

"German, Brazil, France, Ugandan . . ."

"Yes, yes. First, let's make it out of this alive."

Mohan was not yet ready to daydream about their life abroad. Gawande had already organized their American visas and booked them on a flight to Vegas, where his associates would set them up in the business of their choice: either a convenience store on the Strip or a shawarma place, it was up to them. After the penguin job, Gawande had told them, they'd best be out of the country. The man who had bumped off Gawande's rival had already been shipped to Vegas that very evening. This penguin gig would get the cops involved, plus animal rights activists, and those activists were irritating creatures, and dangerous—they had nothing better to do than worry about the plight of lions, hippos, moths, and mosquitoes. They would go on and on until Molt got justice.

Waiting in the lineup to see the enclosure, like upstanding citizens, was making Tapas edgy. He shuffled his feet and sang, his song felt more like a complaint—it was so off-key he might as well have been singing about not wanting to pay an electricity bill.

"Shut up," said Mohan.

Tapas shut up.

He and Mohan smiled at the attendant, trying and failing to look normal. Tapas turned his attention to the white tiles, noticing how they sparkled like the bathroom of a five-star hotel. As he and Mohan shuffled a few steps further, they were hit by the sudden blast of the AC.

"They are giving us a 3-D experience," Tapas said. "North Pole type."

"Maa ki aankh," said Mohan. "Just look at those birds. They're torpedoes."

And indeed, the penguins were jetting through the water at top speed, leaving a trail of bubbles. They were having so much fun, it made Tapas think of his childhood with his brothers, how they had chased each other for no reason at all. There was nothing to be gained, and yet the thrill was so real and true.

"There's an elevator that goes up to the office," said Mohan, nudging Mohan, and pointing with a discreet finger.

"Hah?"

"You're not here to enjoy these mutts. Think of how we'll capture one instead."

Tapas examined the elevator. It led to a room right above the penguin glass tank. He knew what Mohan was thinking. Go up there, get someone to let them into the glass tank. Simple. Clean. Effective. No human being, especially an underpaid zoo employee, was going to risk his life for a penguin. Even though, Tapas had to admit, they were damn cute.

"Look," he said, pointing to the monitor that flashed happy Humboldt penguin images to the public. "There are three males and four females. Donald, Popeye, and Mr. Molt. And Daisy, Olive, Flipper, and Bubble."

"We want Molt," said Mohan. "No one else."

"You think Gawande's wife will know the difference?"

"No, but in the paper they will report the name, won't they? What if the papers say that we took Daisy instead? Then we're . . ."

Mohan abruptly stopped talking. A female cop was moving towards him and Tapas. She had been eyeing them for a while now. Mohan was concerned about Tapas. He got super-edgy and idiotic around cops; he hated them with genuine passion. They scared him too, and his fear made him ferocious.

"Just relax and say nothing," said Mohan. "If she asks questions, I will answer."

"But we are just watching these pandas. Is that a crime?"

"Penguins."

"Hah?"

"These are not pandas."

"They're both black-and-white animals!"

Just as the cop was about to ask them something, Tapas did the exact opposite of what Mohan had told him to do. "Mohan," he said, "do penguins have a penis?"

Mohan did not answer. So, it was Tapas's idiocy that would shine today, not his ferocity.

"They don't have any knees," Tapas continued. "Therefore, it would be impossible for them to do it doggie-style."

The cop had heard Tapas, and repugnance showed on her face. But Tapas didn't notice. He was laughing nervously and mimicking a penguin on its knees, trying to go on all fours but unable to, just staying on its stomach instead. Mohan thought it best to get out of there. He placed his arm around Tapas's shoulder, yanking the younger man's neck so hard that Tapas could hardly breathe.

"Not another word," Mohan said. "You hear?"

Tapas let Mohan drag him towards the exit, but as he left he turned his head and caught sight of one of the penguins sliding and pressing its belly against the glass. He wondered if she might be pregnant. The thought of holding one of these slippery beings and taking it out of its cage reminded him of so many things—of his days in prison as a teenager, when he was wrongfully locked up, way before he started the Fatka gang; of his disbelief at being inside even though he had done nothing, he'd just been taking a walk with his friends, one of whom had a gun, which Tapas had not known of; how volunteer groups came to him in prison and tried to counsel him, talk him out of a life of crime, which he wasn't into to begin with, and of how he kept telling them he was good at painting, and if they would just give him some brushes and colouring pencils he would draw the world for them and prove it; and of how once a kid younger than him had vomited and shat at the same time, right next to him, and it was all black, blacker than the arms of Mr. Molt, or Daisy, or whichever penguin this was, and he'd screamed for help until the prison guard came, and all the guard did when he saw the boy was click his tongue, and that was that, the boy was gone, a click of the tongue the final send-off —and what was the use of staying in a country where these things happened, what did India mean, what was Bharat, what was this desh of his, and America was great, and he would sell cigarettes in Vegas, and Red Bull and chips and lottery tickets, and condoms, no problem, and if it meant taking Mr. Molt away from his family, it was okay, it was fine, because Mr. Molt was just like Tapas. They had both been imprisoned for a crime they did not commit.

THAT NIGHT, BAKUL GAWANDE almost could not bear to look at his wife's face. She had never been so beautiful. He watched as she stood in front of the mirror with a blow-dryer. She had just emerged from the shower and her hair was wet, wet with promise the way it had been when he had first laid eyes on her, all those years ago, at the temple. He had asked the purohit who she was, and that was that. It had taken him a while to get her to say yes, because of his reputation—not a don yet, just a goon with a dream—but he was good-looking and quite the conversational-ist, and a simple man at heart. It had worked.

Tonight, she looked just as striking as she had then, and as the hair dryer howled at her, blowing a stream of hot air her way, Bakul wished its nozzle could suck in instead of blow out, suck in all the demented thoughts of her brain. In front of him now was a false beauty, a fake prettiness, and the dahi and chapatis he had eaten only an hour ago gurgled in his stomach, a sign that his and Reshma's future together was curdling. His wife was gorging on grief, and it was making her look more and more attractive even as she was more and more repulsive, and he had a hand in feeding the beast, no doubt; how he regretted giving the order to capture Mr. Molt.

For her part, Reshma wondered if Keshu would recognize her. After all, it had been three months. More than anything, she could not let her son see her as a mess. She applied a bit of kajal underneath her eyes and, lo and behold, the dark circles seemed like distant memories, dark clouds that had already poured down their rain a while ago. She marvelled at how quickly she had recovered. Wasn't that the nature of love itself? It had taken the skeletal remains of a human being, the remnants of grief that could not be called human, to make her alive again. Just the thought of a reunion, and her tissues were rejoicing.

She could tell that Bakul saw new life in her too, as he watched her get ready. She could feel the relief that he felt, and he also felt a small surge of pride that she was the one who was fixing things for a change. She had entered the world again, and —could she say it? should she dare use the word? yes—there was a *dance* inside her.

She threw the blow-dryer on the bed like a girl who was late for a night out clubbing with her friends, and turned to her husband. "I'm ready," she said.

Bakul wanted to say something, but instead he followed his wife out of their bedroom. All the lights were on, and there were no shadows, but the room felt darker than ever.

TAPAS RAN LIKE HE HAD NEVER run before. Of course, he could not run fast, considering the bundle he held in his arms, but he was doing his best. The thing he carried was howling, making formidable sounds. He tried not to look at it, but part of its head kept jutting out of the white bedsheet wrapped around it.

Mohan followed close behind Tapas, facing the penguin enclosure, gun in hand, keeping watch. They had managed to pull it off. It had been ugly and clumsy, but clean at the same time. No lives were lost; no one was hit. No one had expected two men to emerge at midnight, six hours after closing time, and demand a penguin. There was only a single cop on duty; he'd been slumped in his chair as if he was on Baga Beach nursing a cold beer. By the time this cop realized what was going on, Tapas had confiscated his phone and locked him up in a room. Tapas had enjoyed that part. He'd even given the cop a tapli on the head, the kind schoolmasters gave impertinent kids.

It would be a while before the police were alerted, but Lalit was anxious to get away. The penguin enclosure was right next to a side entrance, far away from the main entrance of the zoo, one that gave them access to Mustafa Bazaar. Into its bylanes they would disappear, and take the highway towards Chembur. Lalit had punched the man guarding the entrance —a pudgy weakling whose sole function was to sit in a plastic chair all day—and took his place. He'd assumed an air of lazy indifference while the abduction was happening, but inside he was quivering. This whole caper was like walking barefoot on rotten eggs.

When he saw Tapas and Mohan running towards him with the package in hand, he rushed to the van that was parked right outside the side gate and slid open its door. Mustafa Bazaar was sleepy at night. Most of the timber shops were now closed, except for a few that had small fires on the footpath, where the labourers were preparing their dinners; and the Parsi colony opposite the zoo was always tranquil, no matter what time of day it was. An old woman emerged from its gates and tried to hail a taxi, but none would stop for her. Their shifts done, all the drivers wanted to go home with the same urgency with which Tapas wanted to get to Vegas.

The cry of the creature in Tapas's arms was unbearable—something like a sheep wailing, a broken *baa* that ricocheted inside the van.

Lalit pointed to the container on the back seat—it was one of those things used to transport dogs on planes. Tapas placed Mr. Molt inside, let go of him as though he was contaminated, and bolted the steel door.

Mohan sat next to Lalit in the front, just in case there was trouble.

"Calm the bastard down," said Lalit.

Not only was the sound excruciating, now the thing was thrashing about in its white sheet. Its flippers hit the walls of the box again and again, and this rattled Lalit to such a degree that he kept trying to start the van even though he had already done so. Mohan gently tapped him on the elbow. Out of the three, Mohan was the only one who'd remained relatively calm. With Tapas and Lalit in a state, he'd had no option.

Lalit zoomed off, his hands still unsteady. Noise was filling the van in the way the same reflections fill up a hall of mirrors —with sudden violence.

Mohan turned the radio on, and a Hindi song with drum-beats and Afro-inspired chants added a new layer of sound. He knew this song; it was a remix of a nineties hit. He turned the volume to maximum until the speakers wobbled, but he did not care. Anything to not hear the life in the box.

He glanced over at Tapas, who was scratching his arms and elbows like one possessed. After taking the guns from the mouse, the two of them had hidden in the bushes, until the security guards had finished surveying the zoo. Something must have bitten him there. Or maybe he was having an allergic reaction. Mohan noticed there was a thick rash around Tapas's neck. Perhaps he needed some air, but the windows had to be up or Mr. Molt would spray the buildings of Mustafa Bazaar with his signature sound.

"Call the boss," said Mohan. "Tell him we're on the way."

But Tapas wasn't listening. He could only hear the drumbeats that were pumping in sync with his beating heart.

"Tapas!"

Tapas looked up at Mohan. He took his phone out and dialled. The name on the display said "Purohit." If there ever was a time when divine intervention was needed, it was now. Anything to calm Mr. Molt. A prayer, a song, even a bullet to the chest.

BAKUL WATCHED AS RESHMA SNATCHED the phone from the purohit's hand. Tapas had been asked to call the purohit because Bakul did not want any calls on his own phone. The aftermath of this escapade would be worrisome, no doubt, and what the fuck was he supposed to do with the penguin once it was delivered to his home? How would he eventually separate it from Reshma?

"Where are you?" Reshma asked.

Tapas hadn't been expecting Reshma to answer the phone. "Didi," he said. "We are—"

"Is he safe?"

"Yes, he—"

As if on cue, the bugger sent out his worst cry yet—a genuine yelp that also sounded fake, as if Mr. Molt was a squidgy toy for a dog, the kind of toy that let out a sound when squeezed extremely hard. Was Mr. Molt aware of what was happening to him, Tapas wondered? Did he know that he was being separated from his brothers and sisters? Did he think of them, feel for them? Did he know their names as Daisy and Flipper, or were they sounds to him, or faces and bodies, or smells?

"Is he crying?" Reshma asked.

"Yes," said Tapas. "I think so." They were on the highway now, zooming along. "We will be there in ten minutes," he said.

"Do you have FaceTime?" asked Reshma.

"What?"

"FaceTime! Do you—"

"No, Didi, sorry . . ."

"Put me on speakerphone."

"Why do you—"

"Just do as I say!" she shouted. "And put the phone near his ear."

Tapas looked at Mohan for guidance; all he received was a nod. So Tapas placed the phone near the grille of the box. Molt was thrashing about, still entangled in the white cloth.

But Reshma had started singing. It was a nursery song, a song about a fairy who puts little children to sleep by sprinkling dewdrops on them. Reshma had a lovely voice, she was a true singer, but Molt was far from soothed. He was singing now too, but about what Tapas could only guess. Perhaps it was a song about ice, about freezing water, about happiness in groups, in the wild, about the chilly sensation that crawled over his skin right now as the van hit a bump on the road.

RESHMA COULD NOT SIT STILL. She could not stand, she could not lie down, she could not stop herself from pacing back and forth in the living room. Keshu was entering the elevator, he was coming up, thirty floors, towards her. What would he say to her? What should she say to him? Would it be a wordless exchange, a surge of love so strong between the two that it would create a magnetic force, and no thought would be needed?

She looked at Bakul, who seemed equally excited, equally eager for the reunion. She had never seen him this way before and she took pleasure in his blossoming. The universe worked in the most mysterious ways indeed, she thought. Perhaps, after witnessing this miracle, Bakul would give up a life of crime. But what would he do? Maybe they could have one more child, son or daughter it did not matter. As long as her Keshu had someone to play with, to share with. Bakul was an only child, and it had made him cold and selfish at times. She had sisters, and she wanted Keshu to experience that feeling of warmth she had known growing up, sleeping alongside her sisters, all of them crafted from the same loving cells.

"Bakul, quick," she said. "We need to go to Keshu's room."

"But we need to open the front door."

"Leave it open. They're on the way anyway. I want him to walk into a familiar environment. He loves his room."

She went into her own bedroom and came back with three toques. She had last used them on the trip she and Bakul had taken to Simla. She also put on a puffy winter jacket, and gave Bakul his. To the purohit, she offered a gold shawl.

She led the purohit and Bakul into Keshu's room. Apart from a split AC, there were ten portable air conditioners blasting cold air into the room, ready for Keshu's arrival. His toy train had been arranged in the middle of the room, and his cars and cycles were lined against the wall. She did not want too much clutter, so she had not yet unpacked his books and colouring pencils. She was so glad she had not thrown anything away. She just hadn't had the strength to do it. But now she realized this had been a mother's instinct. She had always known he was coming back.

A thunderbolt went through her rejoicing heart when she heard the sound of the main door shutting. They were in. He was here.

Bakul was joyous, she knew, even though he couldn't handle the cold; he was behaving like a scared bird, his teeth chattering. She went over to the small alcove near the bookshelf and lit an oil lamp. She gave the purohit a glance and he began to chant his prayers. She wanted Keshu to enter his room with a sense of peace. The purohit also held a garland of marigolds and lilies in his hand, but this was for later. Too much too soon would unsettle the little one. There were yellow laddus too, in case he was hungry.

Lalit opened the door to the room.

Tapas and Mohan placed the box on the ground.

Sounds came from the box, but they were the raspy sounds of tiredness. Bakul had his head down. Never before had his men seen him like this, staring at his feet. The priest sang his song with greater volume now, as though he wanted it to break through the ceiling, split the house in two, and shoot straight to the cosmos, where it would find forgiveness.

Reshma positioned herself right in front of the grille.

When Keshu waddled out of his cage, she burst into tears.

THE

TREASURY

OF

SWEETNESS

M ajid remembered the English textbook for two reasons: one, it was thick and red; two, it used to land on his head time and again, thanks to Mr. Binny, the English teacher whose one look could make an army battalion stand at attention. "Majid, you seem to be amused by something," Mr. Binny would frequently say for all to hear. "Look, Majid is dreaming again. Majid, would you care to share your dreams with the class?" But Majid had no dreams. Or what he thought of as a dream—the idea of leaving Bombay, especially Madanpura, the area that he lived in—was not something he wanted to share with Mr. Binny or with his classmates. His resulting silence was interpreted by Mr. Binny as an act of rebellion, and he would glare at Majid with those grey eyes and bring the English textbook down on Majid's head with great force; behind that force was glee, that of a Christian attacking a Muslim. He held the English textbook with such reverence, and gripped it so hard, even the Bible came second. The English language was the Lord, the Saviour, and Mr. Binny its righteous prophet.

But all of that was in the past. Mr. Binny was an old man now. The last Majid had heard, Mr. Binny could barely see and was living in a small room very close to the school. And even though Mr. Binny had been Majid's nemesis throughout his school life, Majid hardly thought about Mr. Binny anymore. Even today, his thoughts were not so much about Mr. Binny, but about that beautiful fat textbook that had once made his brain shake. What had been a weapon he'd needed to shield himself against was now a gentle fragrance in his memory. Perhaps this was a reflection of his own gratitude—a scent transferred straight from his heart to the pages of that massive treatise on English grammar, and—he hoped—to the writers of that manual: Wren and Martin. He had hated those two in school, had loathed their commas and semicolons, but today, as a new immigrant in Canada, he had to admit that without those two brothers, his English would have been non-existent, his chances of leaving Madanpura nil.

Were they brothers? Were Wren and Martin first names, or last? Majid had always thought of them as brothers, but now, upon reflection, that seemed unlikely. Maybe the kinship was in their single-minded purpose. Yes, that was it. Mr. Binny used to remind the class at least once a week: "This book was not written for you. It was written for the offspring of the British officers stationed in India." Then he would scan the class with a cartographer's eye—although that was just an act. He knew exactly what he was looking for: Majid's Islamic head. "Do you know what 'offspring' means?" he would demand. Of course, Majid didn't. He was barely progressing from one year to the next by achieving the minimum passing mark, and if it hadn't been for the kindness of some of his other teachers, he would have failed a grade or two. But in the sixth grade, Mr. Binny was his class teacher, responsible for overseeing his final mark, and Majid's luck had run out. Mr. Binny did not like Majid's ilk, and the fact that Majid lived in Madanpura seemed to be an affront to Mr. Binny. Majid understood why; he himself did not like the violence, the constant threats his father had to face, the way his older sister was teased by gang members, but he could do nothing about it.

Madanpura was a colourful locality—with meat shops, leather stores, barbers, sweet shops, even a Salvation Army—but Mr. Binny saw just one colour: green. He had once whispered in Majid's ear: "You should go back to Pakistan." Majid had been so terrified that he hadn't dared speak to anyone about it. He feared what would happen if anyone in Madanpura found out about Mr. Binny's open hatred—especially his brother Isa, who would surely slice Mr. Binny's throat with a knife, a beautiful comma from ear to neck. Mr. Binny's hatred was partly thanks to Isa. A few years before, Isa had slapped Mr. Binny during the school march past. In front of the other teachers. Isa was thrown out of school, but it didn't matter to him. By then, he was already involved in smuggling gold. This was in the eighties, when the only things that shone brighter than the strobe lights in Bombay's discos were the gold bars that swam their way across the seas from the Middle East to India, lighting the water at night like illuminated sharks. These were holy bricks of gold because they were being used in religious wars, wars that the Muslims of Madanpura were ready to fight. But while the rest of Madanpura was gearing up for conflict with Hindus, Majid was being tormented by a Christian, and he could do nothing about it. Majid was a coward—unlike his brother, who had done something about the threats, the insults, the affronts to their sister. It also meant Isa had become a perpetrator—and in Majid's mind, that made Mr. Binny right, it made him win.

But today was not about Mr. Binny, Majid reminded himself. Today was about appreciating two brothers, Wren and Martin, who had taught him English, no matter how broken. And today was also the one-year anniversary of his sweet shop in Vancouver, one of the most beautiful cities in the world.

Not only had Majid managed to fly away from Madanpura, he had successfully partnered with a Canadian man to start Almirah Sweets. A treasury of sweetness. That's what the word "almirah" signified. It was borrowed from the Urdu word for cabinet, but for Majid it meant a treasure chest of the most delectable delicacies known to man, woman, or beast. Of course, he did not mention the beast part to anyone, but he'd had a dream the night before the shop opened in which a fantastical beast had towered above him, baring its teeth and fangs; Majid had offered it some mawa dessert, and the beast had eaten the delicacy gently, and had blessed Majid instead of harming him. Majid interpreted the dream as a sign that no matter how foreign these shores looked, no matter how threatening its people seemed, his sweets would bring them together. He was known in the neighbourhood as an affable man, liked by people of all nationalities, and he couldn't wait to bring Fatima and his little daughter Ayesha here. They were stuck in Madanpura, but not for long. Allah had been kind to him. Not so much to his brother, Isa. After all the gold Isa had smuggled, he'd ended up getting shot. Isa now sat in a wheelchair all day, dreaming, the way Majid had once done in Mr. Binny's class. Dreams of better days, of winding back the clock, of the gold that had turned his days black.

But today wasn't about Mr. Binny or Isa.

Majid busied himself with what he considered to be his most important task: keeping the glass display case clean. If there were smudges on the glass, it meant there were fingerprints on the sweets; only his own hands had touched the sweets, brought them into this world. He was maniacal about cleaning the glass. He liked Mr. Clean for the job, trusted his blueness, the big shoulders of the man on the bottle. Mr. Clean understood that cleanliness was serious business. If there was one thing that irked Majid, it was customers pointing to a sweet and *touching* the glass. Why did they need to touch? Just point. But he never chided them. In fact, once a man had pointed to the sweets and tried to pick one up, his hand banging against the glass. The glass was so clean the man couldn't even tell it was there. "Cleanliness is next to godliness." That's what Mr. Binny used to say. And even though he had been referring to Majid's atrocious hand-writing as he'd scratched his pen across the page, across Majid's very being, Majid had agreed with the saying. Unfortunately, Mr. Binny didn't apply the same principle to his own heart. Hearts needed to be clean, cleaner than any handwriting. Isn't that what made the heavens clean? Pure thought. With that, Majid closed his eyes, said a short prayer to his Maker, and opened the doors to his treasury.

Who would visit today? Mr. Clark, from only a few blocks away, who had diabetes but pretended he didn't? Or would it be his wife, Amanda, who issued stern warnings to Majid not to sell her husband anything? Amanda acted out of love and Majid never took her words to heart. She was protecting her man, just as Fatima had done with Majid when they'd first met. It was the small gestures he remembered—how she had smiled at him when he lay flat on the ground thanks to a blow from Isa; that smile had said, "I respect you for not being like them." He had made up his mind then and there that this was the girl he would marry. She was the catch of Madanpura, no doubt. Pure thought.

Or would it be Jamshed, the Iranian man who kept speaking of Tehran, and how it was better, *far* better and more beautiful, than Vancouver? "Only during the Shah's time," he would clarify. "We had streams, natural streams coming in from the mountains and going through the city." He said Almirah's sweets reminded him of sweet times. But sweets are not nostalgic things, thought Majid. Sweets are here and now. The present was sweet, especially his present.

It wasn't Mr. Clark or his wife Amanda; it wasn't Jamshed.

Today there was a new face in the sweet shop, and this was a good sign. It meant that more and more people were hearing about Almirah, becoming enchanted by its tales, lured by its scents. And to top it all, the man was a fellow Muslim. Majid smiled more widely than usual. A smile, he thought, represented arms; and an open smile meant open arms. If he could hug all his customers, greet them with a warm embrace, he would. But that was not allowed in Canada. Of course, he would hug only the men. But even then. There were rules of conduct here, and he respected them. Some of these rules were a bit stifling, but these Canadians knew what they were doing. Vancouver was rated as one of the top three cities in the world to live in. There was Melbourne, then Vienna, then Vancouver. And of course, Madanpura came in fourth. As soon as Majid thought this, he chuckled, but the next second he admonished himself. No need to have proud thoughts on his anniversary. There must be nothing to jinx anything.

The man was standing in front of the glass display case, admiring the array of sweets that Majid had placed before his customers. Just as the apothecaries of old made potions and powders for various illnesses, Majid considered himself a modern-day apothecary curing customers through the senses. If the tongue was sweet, he believed, then words that came out of the mouth would be the same; if the stomach was happy instead of growling, the heart would purr. And the colours that he mixed into his sweets made them dazzle the eye in the same way flowers did. Except that these were flowers you ate. When his partner, Mr. Taylor, had interviewed Majid, that's what Majid had told him: "Sir, my sweets are flowers that you eat." And he had seen Mr. Taylor's eyes light up just like this man's were lighting up now, right before him.

Majid never greeted his new customers verbally. Not unless they looked directly at him. He let the sweets cast a spell. If the customer was a regular, that was a different matter. This man was beguiled, no question about it. After a few minutes he looked up at Majid and greeted him.

"As-salaam-alaikum."

"Wa-alaikum-salaam," Majid replied.

What a pleasure to hear Arabic in his treasury. It had been a while, and the sound added more sweetness to the place; deeply embedded in the sound was its meaning: peace be unto you. Peace. Nothing more important. Nothing more beneficial than peace for human beings. That's what Majid had tried to tell his brother, but would Isa listen? Isa was the big lion, and Majid the young, timid sheep. What lion listens to a sheep? Majid felt the smile dissipate from his lips. Why was he thinking about the past so much? Perhaps he had given too much weight to this one-year anniversary. He focused his attention on the customer.

"Hello, my friend," said Majid. "How can I help you?"

"I have been invited for a birthday dinner," the man said. "And I would like to take something with me."

"Where are your friends from?" Majid asked. The man seemed confused by the question. But to Majid it was perfectly apt. "What I mean is, are your friends Canadian or . . ."

"No," the man replied. "They are not from here."

Majid felt the man wanted to say more, but he didn't. He wasn't shy, but there was a sense of decency about him. He was not mild, but gentle.

"I ask because Canadians have a liking for certain sweets of mine, but not others."

"In that case, I will let you decide. It's better that way. I'm in a hurry. I'm still on my shift."

Through the glass, Majid saw a yellow taxi parked haphazardly. That was okay, the lot was empty. The barber next door had mostly foot traffic, and the convenience store on the other side rarely opened on time.

"You a cab driver?" It was obvious, but Majid asked anyway. He wanted the man to speak, to give something back to Majid.

"Yes," said the man. And that was all.

Majid chose the malpua—a fluffy circular delight, a Mughlai version of the Western pancake, but better. Served with thick sweetened milk. "Serve them hot," he said. "But you probably know that."

The man nodded in gratitude. As he was paying, Majid saw the weariness on the man's face. He hadn't noticed it before, not when the man had first walked in. But now, as the fellow reached into his wallet, Majid saw that his hands were dry, with bits of flaking skin, and the wallet itself mirrored the hand, not so much

roughed up as unable to withstand much. He knew what it was
—they reminded him of Isa's hands. The constant rolling of
the wheelchair, the turning of time, the finality of his brother's
condition. How long had it been since he had spoken to Isa?
Almost three months. Each time Majid asked for him, his
brother came to the phone but stayed silent, surly, as if Majid
had been the one responsible for his condition.

"Thank you," said the man.

Majid nodded. He watched as the man walked away, his
legs heavy as if waterlogged. Perhaps he'd had a hard time in this
country. Majid felt he needed to do something. Show the man
that Canada could be generous, *was* generous, a country that had
welcomed beings such as him. The nation had opened its arms
to those who had been shunned across the border as well. In
times such as these, to do so was a religious act, a spiritual act.
The naysayers argued that it was a naive move, that there would
be a price to pay down the line. If their neighbours were showing
a lack of humanity, Canada was showing gullibility. But there
were always naysayers, Majid argued. There were always those
who viewed kindness as weakness. It made him angry. No, he
would be kind.

"My friend," he said.

The man was almost at the door. He turned around.

"I would like to offer you something," said Majid. "Any
sweet you like, free of charge."

"Oh."

Such a simple word, "Oh"—yet it showed surprise, joy, perhaps even confusion.

"It's the anniversary of my shop today, and I want you to
have something on the house."

"You don't have to."

"I have to," said Majid. "I have to."

The man came closer, almost childlike in his walk to the display case. The heaviness in his legs was still there, but his eyes showed a spark of delight.

"I can't," he said. "But I'm grateful for the gesture."

"Please," said Majid. "I will take it as an ill omen if you refuse."

The man seemed to understand. His breath was heavy, and sweat appeared on his cheeks, just above the line made by his black beard.

"In that case, I will accept," he said. "But you must let me offer you something in return. A free ride in my cab any time you want."

A free ride? That seemed odd. Majid wasn't a child. What would he do with a free cab ride?

"Why are you smiling?" asked the man.

"I'm . . . It's just that no one has ever offered me a free cab ride before."

"We can offer only that which is ours, only that which we are good at."

"I'm sorry," said Majid. "I did not mean to offend you."

"It's okay," said the man. "I'm not offended. But I hope Aidah didn't hear you."

"Aidah?"

"Yes," he said. "She can be sensitive."

"Who's Aidah?"

The man looked at his taxi.

"You've named your taxi Aidah?"

"Why not?"

Because it's weird, odd, crackpot. Majid wanted to say those things, especially the word "crackpot." That had been Mr. Binny's word. He'd used it a lot, especially when speaking about the school principal.

"If one man can name his sweets, why can't another name his cab?" the man asked.

"Well said, my friend."

"So you will accept a ride?"

"I will," said Majid. "Now, what can I pack for you?"

As the man moved closer to the glass display case, Majid felt anxious. The man's hands weren't the cleanest, and Majid didn't want that big frame to lean against the glass, much less for palms to touch the glass. He had a memory of his grandfather, who used to clean his reading glasses all day. He would clean and clean with his white handkerchief, then put his glasses on. Then he'd look at Majid and say, "You don't look dirty anymore. You can go tell your mother you don't need to have a bath." The joke had always tickled Majid. Keep the glass clean and the world looks better. That's what his grandfather had taught him.

Majid watched the man's finger. Long and straight, sure of what it wanted.

"I'll take the gulab jamuns," said the man.

"You can't go wrong with those."

As he packed the brown dumplings, Majid realized that this man was good. He was a man of respect; a man Majid would perhaps like to befriend. Or help. He was a man of character, someone his grandfather would have approved of. After all, he had not smudged the glass.

THE CUSTOMER HAD SHARED the name of his taxi, but not his own name. So the next time the man walked in, Majid asked him straight away.

Jalal was his name. He did not offer a last name, and Majid did not need one. I'm Majid, he thought. Maker of Sweets, Adder of Sweetness, Bringer of Coolness to the Stomach. That's what he wanted to say, but he knew his words would be viewed as peacocking.

The next time Jalal arrived, it was late in the evening, when the shop was about to close.

Majid let him in, let him sit and watch as he closed shop. He even gave Jalal a cup of tea, and the choice of whatever else he wanted from the display case—some sweets he did not keep for more than a day. Jalal argued that Majid was making him fat, and his wife would not like it. She was in Vancouver, along with a daughter, Sara. He was madly in love with his wife, he said. He offered that piece of information without Majid asking, and when Majid said it had to be that way, why would it be any other, Jalal replied that to say it aloud was a reminder of his good fortune, a way of offering thanks. Majid liked the idea, so he offered thanks too, by telling Jalal how much he loved Fatima, how she had dared to stand up to the likes of Isa and his cronies, how she had implored the young police officer who was stationed in Madanpura to let Majid go, when Majid had been picked up by the police in connection with Isa. Majid had been questioned regarding Isa's whereabouts, and even slapped around. But he did not squeak, he did not crumble, he simply maintained his innocence. And when young Fatima charged into the police station and spoke humbly and truthfully, the cop, out of shame, let Majid go. If a complaint had been registered that night, he told

Jalal, his Canadian dream would never have come to fruition. If you had a police record, you could not enter the country. Although it wasn't a Canadian dream back then, he quickly clarified. Back then, it was any dream of leaving, a Get Out of Here Dream. Now, he had only one dream left: to bring Fatima and Ayesha to Vancouver. Once that was done, he would praise Allah so much, Allah would have to descend to Earth and request him to stop. But Majid would not.

Majid did not ask Jalal why, even though he had a wife and daughter here in Canada, even though he was so in love with his wife and called her a "garden he woke up to each morning," there was that patch of sadness in him, the way a lung carries a patch, black and tobacco stained. Majid was sure the patch was there, but it was too soon to ask about it. But the patch was what Majid was after. If he could help Jalal get rid of it, he would consider himself a Good Muslim.

Instead, Majid laughed when Jalal asked him why his English was so good. He wanted to tell Jalal that he'd had the best teacher, and by best he meant the worst, because sometimes the line between the two is so thin only time reveals its true nature. Here was Mr. Binny again, creeping his way back into Majid's present. Perhaps Mr. Binny was calling out to Majid, all the way from Bombay, trying to seek forgiveness? In his last days, what else did a man want? Forgiveness from those he had wronged. Majid would gladly give it. He harboured no ill will towards Mr. Binny—or, perhaps, only a little. If Mr. Binny did ever get in touch, Majid would speak to him in a Canadian accent. He had acquired the accent on purpose. It did not roll off his tongue easily, but he slipped in and out of it as if it was a jumper he wore when it rained—if and when required. "Hey, buddy," he would say to Mr. Binny. "No hard feelings." That would get Mr. Binny's goat. No one had ever called Mr. Binny "buddy." The man didn't have buddies. And now he was dying alone, in a small room, with an old calendar on the wall, a calendar where the faces of the students he had wronged appeared instead of dates. In contrast, the days were flying by here in Vancouver, swift and loud, like those annoying seagulls that always seemed to come out of nowhere. They were the equivalent of Bombay's crows.

Majid had noticed that Jalal always referred to the city as Mumbai. This was normal for people who weren't from there. Majid still called it Bombay.

"That was one bad time," Jalal was saying. "The riots in Mumbai."

"Yes," said Majid. "You lose someone?"

"Everyone lost someone," said Jalal.

"My brother lost his legs."

"I'm sorry," said Jalal.

"It's okay," said Majid. "We all come with our own destiny."

"Do you really believe that?"

"In destiny?"

"In the unchanging nature of things? That no matter what we do, things happen?"

Majid had to think about that for a second. He did believe in destiny, but he also believed in free will. In goodness. In the echo that comes to us thanks to our conduct.

"I believe that certain things are destined. No matter what we do, we must encounter them," said Majid. "People, places, moments, events. But then, apart from all that, there is this huge sky, upon which we can write whatever we want."

"Fair enough," said Jalal.

He didn't say more, and Majid sensed it was his lung patch that was beckoning, making him ask questions then making him retreat. Perhaps Majid needed to push and see if Jalal was willing to share something more, something beyond the name of his taxi.

"I think if you do good, you receive good," he said. "But the things that are written, they will come anyway."

This got no reaction from Jalal. He gulped the rest of his tea, smacked his lips, and shook Majid's hand. Majid looked straight into Jalal's eyes, and noticed dark circles, soft black paper upon which something had been written, the very destiny that he was perhaps grappling with.

THE NEXT DAY, WHEN MAJID SPOKE by phone with Fatima, he told her about Jalal. Fatima said she was glad that he was making friends, but he replied that even though he felt a friendship developing, he was simply doing his duty. Relax, Fatima told him. Have some fun. Why do you always act like a saint? This annoyed Majid. It reminded him of one of Mr. Binny's retorts: "You don't fool me with that Goody Two-Shoes act, Majid. I know who you really are." Back then, Majid had wanted to tell his teacher that he wasn't acting, he was just trying to behave himself and get out of Mr. Binny's hair, which was as curly and unruly as his thinking. And now here was Fatima teasing her husband, saying he was trying to get the Canadian Citizen of the Year Award.

There is no such thing, Majid protested, but Fatima claimed there must be, now that Majid had arrived in Canada. Then she handed the phone to Ayesha. Majid told her to study hard, not to watch too much television, but then Fatima came back on and told him that no one watches TV anymore, these youngsters watch their phones instead, and it was only a matter of time before Ayesha demanded one, and when was he going to buy an iPhone for himself so that she could finally see his shop, and Majid himself in his Canadian avatar, and the city at the other end of the world where he promised them happiness and sunsets and snow like barfi? She must have sensed Majid's temperature rising because she told him to relax, which made him relax even less, until it made him laugh.

Finally, Majid asked to speak with Isa, and Fatima went mute.

She had to live with Isa, in the same house, and look after him even though she didn't like him. He hadn't changed much, she always said; but Majid had faith that he would. Why did Majid have to keep asking for him, Fatima protested. Did Isa ever pick up the phone and call Majid? All he did was get high and talk about his smuggling days when people would shake in front of him as though he were a tiger. Some tiger, Fatima said. More like a snail, a man reduced to a crawl. Divine justice.

But he is good with our daughter, Majid reminded her.

Ayesha cared about Isa. She did not see him as a criminal; she saw an uncle in a wheelchair. Perhaps he and Fatima needed to see Isa in that same light. Put on grandfather's glasses. Clean the glass, clean the glass.

Whenever Isa spoke into the phone, he had a horrible habit of clearing his throat. The sound rumbled through the line, a train full of phlegm. It piqued Majid no end, and he knew Isa was doing it on purpose. Grandfather is watching, he told himself. Isa is your brother. He's lost, but he's still your brother.

"So how's everything?" he asked.

"Perfect," said Isa. "Last night, my legs magically reap-peared."

My brother is testing me, thought Majid. And if it is my brother who is testing me, it is Allah who is testing me. Brothers, blood brothers. One shed blood, while the other ran from it.

"I hadn't spoken with you in a long time, so I thought . . ."

"Yes," said Isa. "It's been a while." Then Majid heard him clear his throat again, and spit—hopefully in his spittoon, the able companion that he carried with him wherever he went, which was mostly from his room to the living room and back. He had once asked Fatima to empty out the spittoon and she had flatly refused. He had asked this to upset her, and he had succeeded.

"When are you coming back home?" asked Isa.

"I am home."

"You expect me to believe that?"

"Why not?"

"It's not home unless the butcher and barber have known you since childhood."

From these words, Majid knew that the conversation would quickly develop into something sour. Not that his relationship with his brother had ever been sweet. Isa had the knack for confrontation, and Majid was not in the mood. He was about to say goodbye when a question suddenly popped out of his mouth.

"Isa, have you heard anything about Mr. Binny?"

"That English lund?"

"Yes, our English teacher."

"If he was the teacher, how come *I* taught him something?"

Isa's tone had changed. Majid imagined him sitting up in his wheelchair, the way he'd sat up as a kid when he'd heard tales of the underworld. Tales of encounters and deceitful set-ups made Isa's spine stiffen, the way the devil's spine did when he smelled something delicious.

"How hard did you slap him?" asked Majid.

"So hard that the sound rebounded off the church walls and landed back on his cheek. Why do you want to know about that piece of shit?"

"Just thought about him, that's all."

"Think about some chick, some hot gand that you want. What the hell are you thinking of Binny for?"

It was strange how easily Isa called him Binny, and how reluctant Majid was to call him anything but *Mr.* Binny, even after all these years.

"I just wanted to know."

"I can find out," said Isa. "Maybe I'll go slap him again."

"No," said Majid. "That's not why—"

Isa started laughing. "You fool, I'm in a wheelchair. Do you think I still slap people? The only person I slap is myself. All the time. To wake up from this nightmare. But my slaps are too weak for that."

"I'm sorry, I . . ."

"Leave it," said Isa. "You wouldn't understand."

"I do, bhai . . ."

"How can you? You left your family here. To rot with a man like me. What kind of person does that?"

A person who wants to make *you* better. In the hope that you see the love that Fatima and Ayesha are capable of. So that someday, maybe, if you change, I can bring you to Canada as well. It's not your legs that are crippled, it's your mind. Majid wanted to say all these things, but his brain was getting hot. To hell with it, he thought. He was about to give Isa a piece of his mind when the line went dead.

AT LEAST MAJID HAD JALAL. Jalal was turning up regularly at the shop now, always arriving just before closing, and whenever he came, he brought something with him, a gift for his own daughter that he would take home at the end of the shift. The things he got her were quite ridiculous: a key chain with a monkey hanging from it, a pair of plastic sunglasses with the words *Love is* written on the lenses in pink, a pair of earmuffs. Jalal's friend owned a dollar store, and he always gave Jalal things for free. Today, he was carrying a golf ball.

"He gave you a used golf ball?"

"No," said Jalal. "I found this."

"Oh. Where?"

"Near the university grounds. I had gone there to drop someone off, and saw it on the road." He held the ball in his hands, and then weighed it by moving his palm up and down. "It's so bruised," he said. "Made me think."

"About what?"

"Golf," he said. "What else?"

Both of them burst out laughing. Jalal's lung patch wasn't receding, but at least there were signs of a friendship between them. How Majid wished he had this easy bond with his own brother. When they were small kids, the distance between them hadn't been vast—it could be covered in a hop, step, and a jump. But then, within a span of months, that distance had become a sea—Arabian, full of gold.

"What's wrong?" asked Jalal.

"Nothing."

"One minute you laugh, the next minute your face turns sad."

"It's just that . . . Never mind, who am I to burden you with my woes?"

"There is no burden amongst friends."

Majid looked at Jalal. Perhaps, he thought, if I tell him about Isa, he will tell me about his own troubles. And so he began speaking, starting with Madanpura's butcher shops, where knives were stored for the cutting and dispensing of human meat, to the joys of gully cricket, where you drew three chalk lines on a wall and whacked a rubber ball around, to the confusion that had swelled in a young Majid when he was instructed to cheer for Pakistan—not India—during a cricket match, to the solid goodness within the community—the elders, the respect they had for others, their attempts at instilling in boys such as Isa and Majid a tolerance for all religions. Madanpura was a whirlwind of opposites, contradictions, good and not-so good battling it out, calls for prayer being met with calls for violence—but during the time when he was growing up, the lure of gold smuggling and, later on, extortion was just too powerful for some to resist. All of this, Jalal listened to carefully. Nodding here and there, uttering a few clucks with his tongue to show disapproval or commiseration.

When Majid spoke about Fatima and Ayesha, Jalal was especially attentive. Something about family was central to this man, thought Majid. Maybe a window into someone else's family was helping him solve a puzzle within his own. Jalal asked about Fatima's and Ayesha's daily lives, then said with gentle admiration, "Your wife and mine are so alike." Strong, determined, soft, independent. Those were the words Majid would have used to describe Fatima, but he didn't need to. Jalal understood. How synchronistic, Jalal said, that Ayesha and his daughter Sara were almost the same age.

"It's so good that Fatima works," Jalal added. "That's good."

"She has to," said Majid. "The thing is, Isa cannot do much, so she has no choice."

"And is the leather shop far from your home?"

"A five-minute walk."

"And Ayesha—where is her school?"

"It's a place called Clare Road . . . very close to where we live."

"Mumbai sounds like such a maze," said Jalal. "I've been only once—that, too, just days before the riots began. After that, I went to Bahrain for work. And now I'm here."

He said "here" as though he wasn't quite sure where he was, or how he'd arrived. *Here.* It was such a confusing word, in the most magical way. For Majid, at least. Who would have thought, when he'd been a child sitting on that wooden chair of his, waiting for the school bell to ring, that he would one day touch snow, or see someone smile at him for no reason, or watch, stupefied, as a bus lowered itself with such humility, with a gentle exhale and hiss, to accommodate a person in a wheelchair. Why wasn't Jalal feeling the same awe? He had told Majid that he was originally from Chiplun, the halfway point between Bombay and Goa—a place of coconut trees, beaches, red earth, monkeys running around. During the rains, when Madanpura's streets were flooded and the gutters overflowed, spewing forth mulch and plastic bags, in Chiplun you could smell the heavens. The heavens left their mark on the earth for you, said Jalal.

"This leather store," he asked. "Is it called Almirah as well?"

"No, no," said Majid. "It's called Isa's Leather Goods. No deeper meaning there, as you can imagine."

Jalal nodded silently. Silences were like countries, thought Majid, they covered so much ground. This silence was going to be fruitful. He felt certain Jalal was going to share something with him. The mention of the rains, it seemed, was causing something to well up inside Jalal. He was overcome, the way the tide suddenly comes in, rushes over a stony dam, and caresses the coconut trees on the shore, a soft reminder of the power of nature. But then the tide gathers momentum, moves further in, starts invading the land of humans, covering the tin roofs of homes, toppling cycles and carts, all while maintaining its grace and its beauty, reminding us of how little effort it requires to touch us. Humans have the audacity to think of the tide as an invasion, when it is a simple reclamation. Now these waves of sadness were reclaiming Jalal, and he was trying to find cover. He was shifting in his chair, staring at his palms, the three thick lines on his forehead folding into each other, trying to change the shape of his face, which might prevent the waves from recognizing him. There was a beauty to it, thought Majid, the endless struggle of all men in this one man.

But then Jalal did something wrong.

He smiled. To cover up his pain, he smiled. And this made Majid feel silly. No, *silly* wasn't the word. Stupid. Like a dolt. Yes, a dolt. Fatima was right. Or, only half-right. Majid was not a saint; saints were wise, not idiotic. Majid had poured his heart out to Jalal, and now, instead of using the opportunity to do the same, Jalal was resorting to a cheap human trick.

Majid abruptly got up and bid Jalal good night. "I need to close up."

"Yes, I should get going too," said Jalal.

Majid watched as his friend opened the door to his taxi. What was her stupid name? Abida, was it? No, Aidah. Who gives a taxi a name? A dolt bigger than Majid. There was no comparison between naming sweets and naming a taxi. That comparison in itself showed a lack of common sense. How could Majid *not* name his sweets? What would he tell his customers? But taxis—of course, they're all taxis. One and the same. One no different from the other. A sweet is a thing; a taxi is a function. Aidah my foot.

And he had left that golf ball on the table.

Golf. An elitist game if ever there was one. While the world struggled with basic food and housing, ten hungry souls living under one tin roof, these golfers wore white belts and caps and fancy shoes, and strutted around while slaves carried their bags. They made a show of putting balls into small holes, walking over a large expanse of green to the sound of ludicrous claps from spectators, joyless approvals of what was not a sport. It wasn't a sport, it was a game, a mind game that the rich played against the poor. Mr. Taylor, Majid's business partner, played golf. Perhaps Majid should have a word with him, make him aware of the affront it offered.

Calm down, thought Majid. What the hell is wrong with you?

These were not his thoughts. These were Isa's thoughts. They had seeped into his brain over the phone, through wires that had somehow found their way into his human circuitry. He rushed outside and knocked on Jalal's taxi window.

"My friend?" asked Jalal.

"Your ball," said Majid. He did not grip the ball, just held his palm flat out, so that the ball looked like an abomination, an evil egg.

"Oh," said Jalal. "I could have picked it up next time."

"I don't like things in my shop that don't belong to me."

He could hear his curtness, and he was ashamed of it. Where had this meanness been hiding? Had Mr. Binny been right all along? Was Majid a Goody Two-Shoes?

"I can see that I have offended you," said Jalal.

"No, no," said Majid. "It's been a rough day."

"All this talk of home, perhaps?"

"Maybe. I miss my wife and daughter. It's been a year . . ."

"I miss my daughter, too," said Jalal.

"Yes, but you'll be home in twenty minutes."

"No," said Jalal. "I will be home, but I won't get to see my daughter."

"What do you mean?"

Jalal tapped the passenger seat.

"What?" asked Majid.

"Come. Sit."

"I can't leave the shop."

"We're not going anywhere. Just sit. You can keep an eye on the shop from here."

Majid walked round the taxi, opened the door, and sat in the passenger seat. There was a distinct smell in the cab, the smell of something being over-cleaned. Prayer beads hung from the rear-view mirror, and the credit card machine had seen better days. Apart from that, there was nothing special about the car; it was just another "yellow."

Without saying a word, Jalal reached out and flipped the sun visor. Pasted onto the back of the small mirror was a photograph.

A little girl, about five years old, squinting in the sun. There was a pout on her lips, as though she was protesting something. That was all. Jalal didn't need to say more. The sun visor, which was meant to shield him from the sun, had blinded him with pain.

"This is the daughter I can never return to," said Jalal.

Majid stayed silent. He felt shame for judging Jalal, for his ego in thinking that he could help him deal with whatever afflicted him. He crushed the golf ball with all his might, choking it, releasing upon it a quiet fury, the fury of the good and the kind and the righteous mixed with the fury of the religious, the proud, the Goody Two-Shoes. Jalal was so silent, the entire taxi was filled with it; it was a space between two large mountains where stillness reigned supreme. Out of respect, Majid felt he should ask something, say something. But he did not know what. "I'm sorry" was common, more useless than anything, "How did she die?" was too soon, too insensitive. "At least you have another daughter" was the coldness of the mathematician. So he asked the only question that seemed honourable.

"What was her name?" he asked.

"Aidah," replied Jalal.

How futile the names of Majid's sweets now seemed. How irrelevant, how superficial. His sweets—barfis, malpuas, gulab jamuns—were eaten, then expelled. But this name, Aidah, stayed with Jalal forever. He carried it with him wherever he went, and he was carried by it, in it, the way a womb carries a child, because that's what Jalal had been reduced to, an infant cursed with unadulterated pain for the rest of its life.

THAT NIGHT MAJID HAD THE MOST horrible yearning to go back to India, to snuggle up next to his wife and child, and beg forgiveness for leaving them. Even though he had every intention of bringing them to Canada, he was still sorry. He prevented himself from calling Fatima; hearing her voice would only make the feeling worse. But as the night progressed, he felt shivers, the kind he'd felt when Isa first showed him his collection of blades and choppers, and when his grandfather had breathed his last.

He sat up in bed and looked outside. There was nothing to see. Just the shapes of some trees. Even the street lights were weak. He dialled his home number. It rang and rang, but no one answered. He tried going back to sleep. It was of no use. He called again. This time someone did pick up. It was Isa.

Majid asked for Fatima.

"What's wrong with talking to your brother?"

"I just need to speak with Fatima about something."

"About your infidelity?" asked Isa. "You found some pussycat there?"

"It's okay," said Majid. "I'll call later."

"Hold on. I did what you asked me to."

"Did what?"

"I've got Binny's number for you."

"What?"

"That prick is still giving English tuition. Can you imagine? The old bastard is still ordering kids around. And he has a mobile!"

But Majid didn't want his number. What would he do with it? He had just wanted to know if Mr. Binny was alive, and even that wasn't a matter of pressing importance.

"I don't want it," he said.

"Then why'd you ask? Now take it down. Call him and do some dirty talk. That's what I did."

Isa laughed—a distinct cackle that could corrode the healthiest and most self-assured of spirits. Majid knew Isa was fully capable of calling Mr. Binny and talking garbage. He decided to take the number down. Isa would hound him until he did.

"Give my love to him," said Isa. "And tell him I've converted to Christianity."

Majid did not bother asking Isa where Fatima was. How he wished she still had a mobile phone. He had bought her three and she had lost all of them. Left one in a taxi, the other at Ayesha's school, and she was still trying to figure out how the third had vanished from her life. That final one had cracked the first day she had it, the screen jagged and distorted, and Fatima had said it was bad luck, a mirror cracking. So that had been it for mobile phones. Majid had purchased an iPhone for himself a month after he came to Vancouver, but he'd found himself surfing porn within a day or two, and was so disgusted with the images he saw, and the strange raw power they had over him, that he'd discontinued his mobile phone service. Porn was for Isa, not for him. Porn was Isa's way of coping, of projecting his hatred onto the world. He did not blame Isa, though. In that one day of viewing porn—Majid's first time ever—the idea of coveting and relishing women he did not know had not seemed unusual. Majid had wanted to be part of the violent joy. And it terrified him, it was unholy.

The night was turning, things were flashing through his mind, but he couldn't counter them in any way. Thoughts from ages ago, moments long forgotten, such as the one time he had peed in his pants in school and was certain Mr. Binny would sniff him out, or the last time his grandfather had cleaned his glasses, the morning before he died, and how it seemed as if Isa had felt nothing, had showed no emotion upon his demise, whereas Majid had cried and cried, and shuddered at the thought of living his whole life with this brother, and soon that shuddering thought became a shuddering reality because both his parents had died within months of each other. Why were these thoughts coming to him now, in the dark, in the third-most-livable city in the world? Why were the trees outside so still?

Perhaps he needed some time off.

He would speak with Mr. Taylor in the morning and ask him if he could go to Whistler for the weekend. The mountains would do him some good. Mountains were the realms of angels, his grandfather had told him. The younger ones were taught to fly by leaping off peaks, so that they might realize their wings were apparitions and it was faith that was keeping them afloat. Majid might see such angels; they might nourish him. Faith. This—what he was going through, his failure to bring his wife and daughter to Canada, his temptation with porn, his inability to be a good friend to Jalal—it was all a test of faith. He drank some cold water and went to bed. The sun was showing through the curtains, soft light that allowed you to sleep, encouraged you to start again. His heart found some ease, and he sank into a waking dream where Fatima and Ayesha were on board a flight, looking down at the clouds, and he was just below, waiting for them on the ground, his arms wide open.

FOR THE NEXT TWO WEEKS, there was no sign of Jalal. Majid worked with increased fervour. His need for the mountains had dissipated; he had thrown himself into making sweets. Milk and sugar were his life, and a sweet one it was. He discovered more organic colours to pour into his sweets, and when he mentioned this to his customers, they lit up as though he had revealed to them a secret passage from the Quran, or whatever teaching they believed in.

Majid was disappointed with how he had behaved upon learning of Jalal's plight, how he had crumbled and gone dark. Jalal had helped him realize he was not as strong and wise as he needed to be. For Fatima's sake, for Ayesha's sake. A true disciple of Allah was both courageous and compassionate, devout in his desire to change for the better.

So when Jalal finally showed up, Majid was ready.

Jalal entered the shop and sat in a corner, as he usually did. Once Majid was done closing up, he made them both some tea and they sat face to face, like old friends, people who knew each other from a long time ago. They stayed in silence for a bit, and that was good. Majid was the one who broke it.

"I'm really sorry about your daughter," he said.

Jalal waved his hand, in a gesture that was casual and friendly. He was trying to start over, to be light. How brave of him.

"That's life . . ." said Jalal. "That's life . . ." He was slow, deliberate. He stared at his teacup.

Again, Majid could sense that Jalal was going somewhere in his mind, or wanted to. And this time, Majid was prepared. Darkness, sadness—these were the weapons of evil, and those who were good had to shed their inhibitions and combat it. The last time, Majid had absorbed it all, been Jalal's sponge. That was a mistake. He needed to be a wall, a kind and caring wall upon which Jalal could lean.

"I'm about to tell you something," said Jalal. "Something that will be hard to hear. But I implore you, hear me out with a calm mind."

Calmness. The ability to stay rooted in goodness, to have faith, no matter what.

"Yes," Majid replied.

"Brother," said Jalal. "I ask for your forgiveness in advance."

"For what?" asked Majid. "You have just called me your brother. There is no question of forgiveness between brothers."

Majid tried not to think of Isa when he said this. But Isa was not only a different kettle of fish, he was a fish from a different sea altogether. Isa's pain was self-inflicted; this man's pain was real, the pain of the good.

"Speak, brother," said Majid. "I'm listening, and the night is ours."

He had no idea why he'd said that, but it felt right. It was large, magnanimous, and he was feeling that way, as huge as the night, ready to take it all in, the shape of trees, the rain, the birds gliding across the skies.

"I want to tell you how my daughter died," Jalal said.

There was no quiver in his voice—or was there? Maybe it was just the echo of the small shop, its glass magnifying details, especially human ones.

"She was on her way to school," he said. "It was the first time we sent her alone. She used to beg us to let her go alone, pleading that she was old enough, and that is when they decided to strike."

"They?" asked Majid. "What do you mean?"

"Please, brother," said Jalal. "I need you to stay calm."

"I am," said Majid. "Please, go on."

"They had warned me that if I didn't listen, something would happen. I didn't listen," he said. Majid was about to respond, but Jalal held his hand up: "I need you to listen."

Then Jalal reached into his pocket and took out an iPhone. He glided his finger across the screen, sliding it this way and that. Then he pressed something, once, twice, and a sound filled the room —of traffic, of *Indian* traffic, the incessant honking, the revving of motorcycle engines, the weak, empty putter of old Vespa scooters that Bombay still housed. Yes, it was unmistakably Bombay.

"I want you to see this video," said Jalal.

He turned the phone towards Majid, and when he did, Majid's heart felt a jolt. "This is . . . isn't this Madanpura?"

Jalal did not look up; he kept his gaze on the screen.

It *was* Madanpura. And it wasn't just Madanpura, it was the leather shop Majid's brother owned, the leather shop where Majid's wife worked. Why was he staring at Fatima? She was walking out of the shop, her faithful brown bag in hand. And . . . who was this? How had Ayesha grown up so fast? She was tall, so tall.

"What the hell is this?" Majid asked.

"Calm," said Jalal. "Stay calm. The people I work for, they need you to do something."

"What people? Did you film this? What's going on?"

"I'm here, brother. How would I film this?"

"Then who did?"

"The people I work for."

"But who? Who do you work for?"

Jalal took a deep breath, so deep it was for the both of them. "It doesn't matter. What matters is what they want you to do."

"Me?"

"You will carry a suitcase. You will carry a suitcase, one that is in my cab."

"A suitcase?" Majid was uttering words, meaningless words, but his mind was screaming. "This is . . . I'm not comfortable with this. I need you to leave."

"You have to leave the suitcase somewhere."

"What are you doing? What is wrong with you?"

"You do this and then you live your life. But not here. You go back to Madanpura."

"What is this? Who are you, madarchod?"

"Calm, brother. Calm. My daughter was filmed by the same people who made this film. I refused to carry their suitcase. Do you see what I mean?"

"Who are you?"

"I'm Jalal. I'm a father, just like you. And I drive my dead daughter around," he said. "I will take you home. You will get your passport. We will get you a business class ticket tonight. After you have dropped off the suitcase."

"Please, why are you doing this?"

"Because my wife begged me to. Because I need to save my other daughter."

"We can go to the police, we can . . . This is Canada, we are safe here."

"I don't want to own two cabs. One cab is enough."

"But what does this have to do with me? Why me?"

"You remember I asked you if you believed in destiny? And you said, 'Certain things are destined. No matter what we do, we must encounter them.'"

But then, apart from all that, there is this huge sky, upon which we can write whatever we want. Majid remembered saying those exact words.

Now, as if reading Majid's mind, Jalal mentioned the sky. He was stuck on the sky. "The skies are where the real battle is going on," he said. "I have never met the people who killed my daughter. It's all text messages and videos and chat rooms. The real enemy is up there, invisible, deadly, all-seeing. When I refused to do their bidding, they showed me what they are capable of. Now I am their recruiter. I need to make sure you do your job or, as I said, I will own a second taxi. And you, my brother, will go through the pain that very few on Earth can know or withstand."

Majid was so cold that he began to shiver. Jalal reached out and steadied him. Majid recoiled, as though a serpent had touched him. He rose from his chair and breathed heavily down on Jalal.

"Easy, brother," said Jalal. "All you have to do is drop off a suitcase. Aidah will take us there."

"I am not your brother."

"But you are," said Jalal. "We are born from the same circumstance. And we will do anything to protect our children."

Majid's hands were turning inwards, the fingers curling into fists. How he wished Isa were here. But Isa was inside his fists, ready to unleash himself upon this man.

"You are not my brother."

"Am I not? For the rest of your life, who will you wake up with? Who, if you do get a chance to grow old, will you remember? Who will haunt you, who will make your teeth chatter? Only fathers, mothers, and brothers can do this. We are not blood brothers. We are much, much worse."

Majid pounced upon Jalal across the tiny table with a force he had never used but always possessed, a force he had suppressed when it showed up, because of Binny or Isa, because it had promised to override his good self, but now this force delivered the most immaculate punch and flattened Jalal. Jalal did nothing to fight back. He let Majid destroy him, he let the blood flow from his lips, as though it were simply an extension of the threat his lips had just leaked.

"If someone sees us, they will call the police," said Jalal. "And that's the last you'll ever see of your family. Please, I beg you."

There were tears in Jalal's eyes. Majid stopped. He sat. He felt an overwhelming urge to call someone. He wanted to speak with Fatima. Or even Isa would do. Isa was great in a crisis. Especially when there was blood involved. Majid was panting, ribs expanding and contracting like those of the pye-dogs that lived in his old lane, those angry, scared night-howlers.

"I . . . What's in the suitcase?" he asked. His voice was quiet.

"I don't know. And it's better if you don't either."

"If I do this, how will I know they will leave me alone?"

"They keep their word, both good and bad."

"But . . . I will be sinning, this is not the way."

"It's the only way," said Jalal.

"But what about the shop? Mr. Taylor, he . . . he showed so much faith in me."

"So did Aidah. She showed faith in me, and I let her down. My wife did not speak to me for a year. One day when I got home, she had written a word on the wall. It broke my heart to read it."

"What word?"

"Don't let Fatima write that word on the wall."

"What word?"

"We must leave now. I'm afraid there is nothing else to do."

"But Allah . . ." Majid wanted to say more, but his mouth was dry.

The Almighty is all-knowing, all-seeing. Surely He was capable of intervening. Could it be that Majid was not deserving of His protection? He had watched porn, he had laid eyes on the breasts and thighs of women, women who showered their cheap affection on any man for the world to see. He had encouraged them, joined them in their glee. He had judged Isa, a brother, a real brother, for being violent, inhuman, and now he himself was about to do the most inhuman of things. He had never forgiven Mr. Binny for torturing him, and now he envied Mr. Binny, his small room and the days to come—there were so few of them left, but Majid's days felt like a piece of land racing towards the horizon, never catching up. If only he had called Mr. Binny and forgiven him, maybe things would have been different.

"But this . . . this is against the Quran . . ." he said.

"What makes you think these people are Muslim?" asked Jalal.

Majid felt as if he was choking. He needed air.

It was Jalal who let him have that air, Jalal who escorted him outside. Majid threw open the doors to his shop and stood in the empty parking lot. The barber next door had gone home to his family. How beautiful that must be. Majid looked up at the sky, where his destiny had been written by men he did not know, men whose orders and intentions were travelling across the sky right now, silent and undetected. Messages from one keyboard to another, one country to another, the true keepers of the planet. They were farishtay, but apostles of the dark. He saw a star appear, then another, then a third. They were revealing themselves to him, new constellations were being born right before his eyes, the constellations of his wife and child. How he wished he could have his grandfather's glasses this very moment. Things wouldn't look so real and scary then. He would clean the glass, clean the glass. He would put them on, he would stare at the sky, and perhaps another star would appear, for people like him, a star where he could buy time, appeal to a higher power, consult with better apostles, apostles who would show him the way home, tell him to open the suitcase because it was empty in the end. Or perhaps, he thought, Aidah, now reborn in the realm of love, would ignore her father's hands on the wheel and drive both men to safety, to a place between the mountains, where the constellations did not work, where the signals were unable to reach, where two brothers sat in silence and waited for the real angels to come.

DEPARTMENT OF IMMIGRATION CIRCUS · BYCULLA (MUMBAI)

VISA

2012 JAN 07

F 047

DEPARTMENT OF HOME AFFAIRS

VISA

2011-02-12

TFG

DEPARTMENT OF IMMIGRATION AND BORDER PROTECTION

ADMITTED
TOS

MAY -2 2009

04

1809

Class

Until

VISITOR
VORGATE PARK
06/08/01

TRANSLATED

FROM

THE

GIBBERISH

PART TWO

As my time to leave India approaches, my heart starts beating differently. It pulses with the knowledge that I'm going home, and leaving home, at the same time. Of course, I will come back again, but for now I must ready myself for another year in Canada. What is it that gives immigrants arrhythmias? Is it knowing that each time my plane lands in Vancouver, my feet never touch the ground? It is said that sexual identity exists along a spectrum; so does coming home. One day I am kind of home, the next I am somewhere in the middle, the third I am staring at the deep end.

Two more days to go.

Sleep is irrelevant now. I start jet-lagging before I change time zones. Melatonin has no power compared to exile.

I lie in bed, feel the sheets turn into water again.

I start doing my first lap, but now I notice a man who is floating on his back. I notice his lungs, in particular. They are charcoaled with cigarette smoke, and around them, a black dye is being released in the water. His lungs are signing his last will and testament in the pool, and we who watch are all his notaries, but no one is taking the job seriously. I get out of the pool and give sleep a shot, the way you would a former lover.

I fall asleep early for a change, and I have a dream. An Indian dream.

I'm an Indian king, asleep in my bed in ancient India. I'm being fanned by giant leaves, Indian leaves, but soon those leaves turn into pine and fir and maple, and I wake with a jolt. It's only 2 a.m. The night is still young and I am growing old, so old. I go to the window again and stare at the playground. I still haven't discovered why I want to write about it. Right now it's a silent mixture of earth and iron—mud, swings, and jungle gyms. A story will grow from it, I know.

Dr. Hansotia is still ignoring me. His wife's underwear isn't. It's the flag of a nation now, such is its power, its silence. I think of Jaloo aunty. When I was a kid, she was the one who taught me to make chai. Isn't that strange? I had gone to her home to tell her that Yezdi was crouched underneath the stairway, three floors below, crying. We were all playing hide-and-seek, and he hid there, and it was my turn to seek, and when I found him, he was already crying; when I asked him what was wrong, he didn't respond, and when I gently touched him on the shoulder, he yelped and winced. Could she go down and fetch him? I didn't want the other kids to find him. They'd make fun of him. She nodded, and asked if I would watch the tea she was boiling.

I didn't count on the milky, frothy liquid rising. I had been told to *watch* the tea, but what could I do about it rising? I had never even entered the kitchen at my own place. As the tea rose, more volcanic by the second, I took a pair of tongs and lifted the pan. I didn't turn the stove off; I just kept putting the pan on until the tea frothed, then taking it off again—a method I use to this day. It's weird how something you do every day is connected to someone who is so far away from your present.

When Jaloo aunty came back up that day, Yezdi went straight to his room.

"What's wrong?" I asked her.

"Nothing," she said. "My son is . . ."

Then she trailed off, the way you walk in a forest and the path just disappears. It leads nowhere. She looked at me with tenderness. She patted my head. She wanted to say more. I wanted to hear more. It was the first time I had connected with a woman her age who was not a relative. Suddenly, the distance between us wasn't vast. I felt that she was just as old as I was, and I was just as old as she. She was hurt, or perhaps scared, the way strong people get scared when they realize something is out of their control.

"Do you know how to make tea?"

"No," I said.

"Would you like me to show you?"

"Yes, Jaloo aunty."

I don't remember much else from that conversation, but I do remember her telling me exactly when to put the lily chai in, how long to boil it for, when to add sugar, and so on. We both were silent as she made the tea again, this time especially for me. "Now *you* strain it," she said. I held the strainer in one hand and picked up the vessel with the tongs. Making tea is something I do even today when I am stressed out. I take out tongs, and watch the residue remain as the liquid goes below and the fragrance rises above, available then gone.

Jaloo aunty and I drank our tea in silence. It was my first cup of tea in a long time. I had had it last in Kashmir, when I was three. I remember standing on the balcony of a hotel, sipping from a red plastic cup. After that day, Jaloo aunty and I never spoke at length again. On the rare occasion that I went over to her apartment—I visited once or twice to give Yezdi comic books —she barely acknowledged me.

Now I want to share this with Dr. Hansotia. Three a.m. seems like an appropriate time for us both. One man nearing the end of his life, approaching a deep sleep; the other in his forties, trying to sleep. Sleep, when it comes, is so delicious for me, like ice cream, or a naked body, or a great piece of literature. Sleep is my god, the one to whom I pray, the one who will never show itself. Sleep is androgynous, that beautiful long shadow, a precursor of death, who will come one day for sure, but never at your convenience.

This time, I ring the bell.

This time, I announce my arrival.

The meaning is clear: I'm not here to offer my condolences.

Dr. Hansotia opens the door. His stomach peeps out at me. It seems to lead the way. "Son, it's late," he says.

"I just wanted to see you. I'm leaving tomorrow," I say.

He thinks for a second. Then he opens the door wider and I slip in. But I had already slipped in. I was sitting on the sofa while he was still at the door. The house has that same peculiar smell I remember, the doctor's smell. We sit across from each other. The bookcase is still there. I cannot tell if Mr. Williams is, too.

"I hear you've become quite well-known in Canada," Dr. Hansotia says.

"Not really," I say.

I don't know what to make of my own average well-knownness. On some days it feels like a legitimate thing; on others, it is ridiculous. To be known. For one's work to be recognized. Awarded, rewarded. Critiqued, criticized, analyzed, cauterized.

"I haven't read any of your books," he says.

"That's okay," I say.

I'm used to it by now. No one in my family reads my work either. They buy my books as gifts to give to others, as one would a T-shirt or a perfume. What's a book, anyway? What is a novel? Labour + blood + deep thought + carpal tunnel. No wonder people prefer T-shirts. What is a short story collection? Writing about characters who don't deserve novels. Lives so insignificant that they can be summed up in a few pages. I would be a short story; so would Dr. Hansotia. We are two short stories facing off, staring at each other, wondering how we could become novels. No wonder authors write memoirs. In a memoir, you can stretch your own significance.

"I'm sorry about Jaloo aunty," I say.

He nods. He sighs. He says nothing.

"Why didn't Yezdi come for the funeral?" I ask.

This takes him aback, awakens him. To him, I am still that little boy, a young man with a deviated septum. Only a wolf would ask such a question, a wolf that is biting sleep, chomping its jaws on something he will never catch, and so is hungry for everything else.

"I'm sorry," I say. "I didn't mean . . ."

He waves his hand; it's okay. At least, that's how I read the gesture.

"I liked Jaloo aunty," I say.

"You are the only one who has asked me that to my face," he says. "The others have asked too, but with sweetness and embarrassment."

"It's just that . . . why wouldn't he come for her funeral? It's his mother."

"Exactly," he says. "I'd expect him to not come to mine."

"I'm sure you were a good father," I say.

"I'm not his father."

"What do you mean?" I ask. He sees the glow on my face, how he has provided some meaning to my visit with him, perhaps to my visiting India, even.

"She had an affair during our courtship. It didn't stop me from loving our son, but it stopped her."

"Did Yezdi know?"

"He found out. It had an impact. She saw him as a sign of her infidelity. I even offered to step out of the way."

"I don't know what to say."

"There's no need to say anything."

But . . . why the underwear? I want to ask, but that would make me just as pedestrian as everyone else. What does it mean? Is it to embarrass others, to make her infidelity public? To send her a message in case her spirit is watching? Am I reading too much into an undergarment?

"Anyway, I must be going," he says. Then he gets up and goes into his room. He leaves me in the darkness of the living room, sunk in an old sofa that smells of disinfectant.

I get up, I walk towards the door. But then I go back inside. I sit on the sofa. It's black and leathery. There are small patches on it, bits of skin that have been ripped out. I lie down on the sofa and close my eyes.

LEAVING

I dump things into two suitcases. Books, shoes, clothes, belts, socks, some medicine that someone has asked me to carry for them—a head balm or painkiller that is either unavailable in Canada or too expensive. Along with my carry-on, I take a neck pillow that reminds me of a toilet seat. When we humans fly, we wear fluffy toilet seats around our necks.

Friends come over to visit me and offer their condolences, as if my going back to Canada means I will freeze there, or I will get lonelier and therefore more irredeemable by my next return. There is pity in their eyes as well, for I will not be here for a particular wedding, or a trip to Goa, or a wild night out at a club; I will be unable to randomly meet people at midnight if I feel like having a coffee. That's the beauty of Bombay—someone you know is always awake. But I tell them the usual: man, it's too polluted here, it's too chaotic, it's so this, so that . . . Then why do you keep coming back? they ask. To remind myself, I say, of what I'm not missing. Of what I've thankfully left behind. They don't believe me, and even though I'm a good storyteller, I'm unable to weave a story for myself, one that I can get lost in, and never emerge from.

Saying goodbye to my parents is always hard. When I was a kid leaving the house to play football or cricket, I used to rush out the door. I was a tiny tornado who couldn't wait to leave. Now I trudge along, pretending it's the heaviness of the suitcases that is causing slowness. But no one ever stops me. Life goes on. Things keep turning. It would perhaps make sense if the world stopped, just for a millisecond, to help us feel a little less insignificant. But then again, this idea of finding meaning is what needs to be abandoned. Leaving is the ideal way to embrace your obsoleteness.

That's what airports are—lines and lines of people checking in to register their obsoleteness. And that's what airport lounges are: incubators of the sickness, built to exacerbate the condition. Once at Heathrow Airport I had a nine-hour wait, to go to either Bombay or Vancouver, I don't remember and it doesn't matter, and I slept in a corner of the business-class lounge. I had used my miles to get an *upgrade*—that thing that makes us feel like gods—and I started to fall asleep, began to taste the deliciousness of it. When I woke up an hour later, an Indian couple, elderly, kindly, was staring at me. Before I could orient myself, the woman said to me, "You sleep exactly like my son." There was a smile on her face, and her husband went back to his newspaper. I had the distinct feeling that their son had died. She looked at me with such longing that I felt compelled to ask, but I didn't. I just smiled back, then got up and left. Two people, feeling obsolete without their grown son, incubating in sorrow and business class regret. Back then I could still sleep.

I have been handed my boarding pass. My entry into the tunnel has been granted. I am a verified escapee, who will soon descend onto a plane that is actually a tunnel that is really a large MRI machine, scanning our insides while we stay half-awake, registering minor tears and cracks, and bulging discs that impinge upon nerves and send signals of pain straight down our thighs to our feet—because once again the land we land upon is not ours, and never will be.

✈	BOARDING PASS	BOARDING PASS

NAME: ANOSH IRANI

FROM: BOM-PEK   DATE:

TO: PEK-YVR   CLASS:

GATE: FLIGHT Nº: BOARDING TIME: SEAT:

NAME: ANOSH IRANI

FROM: BOM-PEK

TO: PEK-YVR

DATE: TIME: CLASS:

GATE: FLIGHT: SEAT:

There it is—a validation of my condition, a reminder of my mistakes. Of promises I was unable to keep, loved ones I was unable to look after. Suddenly, the boarding pass transforms itself from paper to electronic, and I'm holding a screen in my hand, and it flashes news and headlines the way Reuters does in green, at Times Square:

You weren't there when your grandmother died of cancer in your room . . . you left people you loved . . . you ran away from land your forefathers owned . . . you became moody and against life . . .

And then the statements become more and more accusatory, related to things I didn't do, have no knowledge of, that aren't related to me in the slightest, but they are being directed my way, transmissions meant for another immigrant, someone in another lounge, but perhaps they have anaesthetized themselves to the headlines, they are fine, but I am the interloper, the one in search of answers, and they come hard and fast my way, and it does not matter if they aren't mine:

Where the fuck were you when Daddy died? . . . you just left, you didn't think of asking me to join you . . . you don't deserve to be called a daughter . . . you get a raise and you stop sending money . . . fuck your lawn, the weed is you . . . listen, we can start a business together . . .

brother, please get me out of here . . . sister, don't marry him, he's no good . . . son, today your father forgot my name . . . I'm so sorry, but she died last night . . . where are you, call me, call me, call me . . .

I don't know whom to call, whom to tend to. I try moving forward.

When I am in my seat, I think of the things I need to do once I land.

The house will smell of emptiness, the mail will have to be sorted out, vacuuming, dusting, oh, look, someone stole my garbage bin, and then the horrible beast of jet lag, providing sleep and then taking it away, and then . . . then what? . . . back to the same . . . a new story, a new play, a new grant application . . . but what is the thing behind the thing?

I stare at the boarding pass. It has turned back to paper, back to something material, and it occurs to me that this is the problem. I am too physical. I need to see myself from afar, everything from miles away. I get myself a new boarding pass.

BOARDING PASS		BOARDING PASS		
NAME: ANOSH IRANI		NAME: ANOSH IRANI		
FROM: BOM	DATE:	FROM: BOM		
TO: OUTER SPACE	CLASS:	TO: OUTER SPACE		
		DATE:	TIME:	CLASS:
GATE: FLIGHT Nº:	BOARDING TIME: SEAT:			
		GATE:	FLIGHT:	SEAT:

I don't need an airplane because I am a writer, a combustible being, a flammable object. A rocket. I feel a tremendous amount of heat, my nerves are on fire, they are singing hallelujahs, they are chanting *oms*, they are sending out the sweet ring of temple bells, they are incanting the gathas of Zarathustra, they are millions of muezzins sending out a call for prayer, they are feverish and erotic, they are going back centuries and pulling whatever strength they can from both believers and heretics, from the algae and the dinosaurs, because all are in search of the same thing behind the thing, and I lift off, I implode, my heart eats itself as it has been created to do, and a beautiful nothingness envelops me.

I am both awake and asleep, in both womb and sky at the same time, and I can see what we call Earth from a great distance, this ball that we feel entitled to. At first, space feels uncomfortable. I find it hard to steady myself, so I keep spinning, and the Earth remains frustratingly still. But then I realize that this is nothing but black water, and I am in a pool, a large public pool, with a population of one. I start cycling my arms and legs, I do the crawl, and I am stable.

I look at this place from a distance, I try to see its beauty, but I cannot.

It looks quite fragile to me, this round ball on which I am held captive. Fragile, but not in a tender way. It is not a healthy, vulnerable fragility. It is something else, and before I can find the correct sentiment for it, I see an old man a few feet away from me, staring at it the same way I am. I recognize him immediately as that diagnostician Hermogenes. He and I don't speak at all, but his presence tells me all I need to know about Earth—this body is breaking too; it is decaying just like any human. And water, that eternal truth-teller, is once again surrounding us, flooding, tsunami-ing into our bodies, but no one wants to listen.

I didn't either; I did not know how.

Have I come all this way to find out that we are a failed species? Is our failure that thing behind the thing? Possibly. But I keep looking. Might as well, since I'm here.

I gaze down at Dr. Hansotia's clothesline. And what I see pleases me. The first rains of the season have come on the day I leave. There has been a downpour, and what else but water—this time, from the skies—can solve the matter of the undergarment? It hits the garment again and again, lashes against it, cleans it, until it is wet with truth, and somehow falls, even though it shouldn't, even though its heaviness should cause it to droop and hang more. It falls and lands on the hood of a parked car. I doubt Dr. Hansotia will hang it up again.

I see Canada, too. I see it for what it truly is—the cause and the balm.

What else do I see? The usual. It's really what all of us see on the news.

Hezbollah, Gaza, ISIS, untouchability, the imaginary wall, some small child carrying water for his choleric mother, Manchester United versus Real Madrid, bombs—both massive and Molotov—an Alaskan cruise, a baby penguin taking its last breath in the Mumbai zoo, some writer in the mountains of Banff trying to find the perfect internal rhyme for a poem, illegal immigrants burrowing through the earth and causing tectonic plates to shift, people meditating and gardening and joining pottery classes, parents dropping kids off at hockey, some kid expert at wiring stealing electricity in a slum, under-age sex slaves entombed in boxes for hours at a stretch, over-age sex slaves too afraid to disobey pimps, a production of *A Streetcar Named Desire* in Turkish, people screaming at the people who have wounded them hurt them betrayed them falsely maligned them trapped them, it's all there, all at once, and in the middle of it all the ice caps melting, water unfreezing, thawing, showing its empathy.

I believe in reincarnation. But I pray it isn't true.

Life is so generous, and so bountiful in its pain. I do not wish to come back to this planet, to bask in its unforgiveness. I accept that I have been unable to grow, to make that leap from human to something smaller, simpler, gentler, a living organism quietly content to contribute to the planet in exchange for a small corner. If writing is about truly seeing, then so is living. Complete annihilation is the only way forward for me. For my troubling "I."

But then . . . haven't I failed too? Again?

This must be why the world is round. Roundness is what we have given it through our mistakes, circular and repetitive. Those who came before us created that shape, and we are experts at maintaining it.

I see a mass of humans, all flailing as they swim—towards offices and jobs, towards terrorist cells, towards people and away from them, towards husbands and wives who love them but long for someone else, towards children who may never show up when they die. If I leave, if I combust like the flammable object that I am, am I not flailing too?

Perhaps all I can do is return, and bring some kindness and humour to this soil, so that when I am reduced to bone the worms will eat what remains—but not before I shed my grudges, my hate, and my frustration. For if the worms cannot taste my forgiveness, they will be unable to pass on traces of my humour, or wisdom, or any shred of my intelligence.

But then again, I tell myself, endings aren't about redemption. There is no redemption for us. Perhaps there's only a small movement towards healing, a sparrow step, the way a baby curls its tiny palm around your finger and gives its entire being to you, without even knowing who the hell you truly are.

ACKNOWLEDGEMENTS

I am grateful to the Canada Council for the Arts and the British Columbia Arts Council.

Thank you to my colleagues in the World Literature Program at Simon Fraser University—Melek Ortabasi, Ken Seigneurie, Azadeh Yamini-Hamedani and Mark Deggan—for your support over the years. Thanks also to David Chariandy for always being so helpful.

Thanks to Madeleine Thien, Rawi Hage, Aislinn Hunter, David Staines, Anna Rusconi, Rachel Ditor, and Karthika VK for reading earlier versions of some of these stories with so much care and generosity.

Thanks to Neera Agnihotri and Rajesh Mansukhani for your guidance on "Behind the Moon" and "Butter Chicken" respectively.

Thanks to Kristin Cochrane, Louise Dennys, Anne Collins, Rick Meier, Jennifer Lum, Deirdre Molina, Max Arambulo and everyone at Knopf Canada for championing my writing and being such a pleasure to work with.

My gratitude to Karolina Sutton and everyone at Curtis Brown. Your time and efforts are much appreciated.

Thanks to Medaya Ocher and Erika Recordon at the *Los Angeles Review of Books* for publishing "Behind the Moon"; to Madeleine Thien, Catherine Leroux, Francisco Vilhena and Luke Niema for publishing "Swimming Coach" in *Granta*; and to Curtis Gillespie for publishing "Circus Wedding" in *Eighteen Bridges*.

ACKNOWLEDGEMENTS

Thank you to Boman Irani for the author photograph and for always making time, no matter how busy you are.

And, finally, to my editor, Lynn Henry, for your faith, vision and guidance—I say the same things again and again, but only because they're true.

ANOSH IRANI has published four critically acclaimed novels: *The Cripple and His Talismans* (2004), a national bestseller; *The Song of Kahunsha* (2006), which was an international bestseller and shortlisted for Canada Reads and the Ethel Wilson Fiction Prize; *Dahanu Road* (2010), which was a finalist for the Man Asian Literary Prize; and *The Parcel* (2016), which was a finalist for the Governor General's Literary Award for Fiction and the Writers' Trust Fiction Prize. His play *Bombay Black* won the Dora Mavor Moore Award for Outstanding New Play (2006), and his anthology *The Bombay Plays: The Matka King & Bombay Black* (2006) and his play *The Men in White* were both shortlisted for the Governor General's Literary Award for Drama. He lives in Vancouver.